*Life is a game of power and pleasure.
And these men play to win!*

Let Modern Romance™ take you on a jet-set journey
to meet eight male wonders of the world.
From rich tycoons to royal playboys—
they're red-hot and ruthless!

International Billionaires coming in 2009

The Prince's Waitress Wife
by Sarah Morgan, February.

At the Argentinean Billionaire's Bidding
by India Grey, March.

The French Tycoon's Pregnant Mistress
by Abby Green, April.

The Ruthless Billionaire's Virgin
by Susan Stephens, May.

The Italian Count's Defiant Bride
by Catherine George, June.

The Sheikh's Love-Child
by Kate Hewitt, July.

Blackmailed into the Greek Tycoon's Bed
by Carol Marinelli, August.

The Virgin Secretary's Impossible Boss
by Carol Mortimer, September.

8 volumes in all to collect!

Dear Reader

When I was invited to write one of the books in Mills & Boon's rugby series I was seriously thrilled. I grew up in a family where rugby was a passion, and from a very young age would go with my dad and my older brother to Murrayfield to watch Scotland internationals. Of course at the time I wasn't old enough to fully appreciate those magnificent, muscular men, but I guess they must have made a pretty lasting impression, because when I began to write my first Mills & Boon® novel at the grand old age of thirteen it featured a hero who was a rugby player!

The book never got finished, and I've long since lost the manuscript (handwritten, in a blue exercise book), but I've never forgotten the hero, with his aura of constrained power and intense focus. Having the chance to reincarnate him in the form of brooding Argentinean Alejandro D'Arienzo was a bit like rediscovering my first love.

Rugby is such a hard, sexy game. It demands not only phenomenal physical strength (mmm...hold that thought...) but huge amounts of courage and mental endurance, which I think are all essential ingredients for the perfect hero. My heroine, Tamsin Calthorpe, would definitely agree; she lost her heart to Alejandro when she was just fifteen years old, the first time she set eyes on him out on the rugby pitch. Now, after nine lonely years, she'd actually quite like it back, so she can move on with her life... The trouble is, rugby players are also driven to win at all costs—and Alejandro's not going to give up anything without a fight!

This book was such a lot of fun to write—especially the day I spent at Twickenham with two of the lovely editors from Mills & Boon, seeing some of the places that feature in the book. It was great for research, but not so good for my mud and muscle obsession. Oh, dear. Time to rush off for my meeting at Rugby Players Anonymous...

India

AT THE ARGENTINEAN BILLIONAIRE'S BIDDING

BY
INDIA GREY

MILLS & BOON®
Pure reading pleasure™

First published in Great Britain 2009
Harlequin Mills & Boon Limited,
Eton House, 18-24 Paradise Road, Richmond, Surrey TW9 1SR

© Harlequin Books SA 2009

Special thanks and acknowledgement are given to India Grey

ISBN: 978 0 263 87007 7

Set in Times Roman 10 on 11 pt
01-0309-57168

Printed and bound in Spain
by Litografia Rosés, S.A., Barcelona

A self-confessed romance junkie, **India Grey** was just thirteen years old when she first sent off for the Mills & Boon® writers' guidelines. She can still recall the thrill of getting the large brown envelope with its distinctive logo through the letterbox, and subsequently whiled away many a dull school day staring out of the window and dreaming of the perfect hero. She kept those guidelines with her for the next ten years, tucking them carefully inside the cover of each new diary in January, and beginning every list of New Year's Resolutions with the words *Start Novel*. In the meantime she also gained a degree in English Literature from Manchester University, and, in a stroke of genius on the part of the gods of romance, met her gorgeous future husband on the very last night of their three years there. The last fifteen years have been spent blissfully buried in domesticity, and heaps of pink washing generated by three small daughters, but she has never really stopped daydreaming about romance. She's just profoundly grateful to have finally got an excuse to do it legitimately!

Recent titles by the same author:

TAKEN FOR REVENGE, BEDDED FOR PLEASURE
MISTRESS: HIRED FOR THE BILLIONAIRE'S PLEASURE
THE ITALIAN'S CAPTIVE VIRGIN
THE ITALIAN'S DEFIANT MISTRESS

For my dad (1940–1981) who loved rugby so much,
and for my mum, who supports me with the same
unfailing enthusiasm as she supports Scotland.
With love and thanks.

PROLOGUE

TAMSIN paused in front of the mirror, the lipstick held in one hand and the magazine article on 'How to seduce the man of your dreams' in the other.

Subtlety, the article said, *is just another word for failure.* But, even so, her stomach gave a nervous dip as she realised she hardly recognised the heavy-lidded, glittering eyes, the sharply defined cheekbones and sultry, pouting mouth as her own.

That was a good thing, right? Because three years of adoring Alejandro D'Arienzo from afar had taught her that there wasn't much chance of getting beyond 'hello' with the man of her dreams without some drastic action.

There was a quiet knock at the door, and then Serena's blonde head appeared. 'Tam, you've been ages, surely you must be ready by—' There was a pause. 'Oh my God. What in hell's name have you done to yourself?'

Tamsin waved the magazine at her sister. 'It says here I shouldn't leave anything to chance.'

Serena advanced slowly into the room. 'Does it specify you shouldn't leave much to the imagination, either?' she croaked. 'Where did you get that outrageous dress? It's completely see-through.'

'I altered my Leaver's Ball dress a bit, that's all,' said Tamsin defensively.

'That's your *ball dress*?' Serena gasped. 'Blimey, Tamsin, if

Mama finds out she'll go mental—you haven't altered it, you've *butchered* it.'

Shrugging, Tamsin tossed back her dark-blonde hair and, holding out the thigh-skimming layers of black net, executed an insouciant twirl. 'So? I just took the silk overskirt off, that's all.'

'That's *all*?'

'Well, I shortened the net petticoat a bit, too. Looks much better, doesn't it?'

'It certainly looks different,' said Serena faintly. The strapless, laced bodice of the dress, which had looked reasonably demure when paired with a full, ankle-length skirt, suddenly took on an outrageous bondage vibe when combined with above-the-knee net, black stockings, and the cropped black cardigan her sister was now putting on over the top.

'Good,' said Tamsin firmly. 'Because tonight I do *not* want to be the coach's pathetic teenage daughter, fresh out of boarding school and never been kissed. Tonight I want to be…' She broke off to read from the magazine. '"Mysterious yet direct, sophisticated yet sexy".'

From downstairs they could hear the muffled din of laughter and loud voices, and distant music wound its way through Harcourt Manor's draughty stone passages. The party to announce the official England international team for the new rugby season was already underway, and Alejandro was there somewhere. Just knowing he was in the same building made Tamsin's stomach tighten and her heart pound.

'Be careful, Tam,' Serena warned quietly. 'Alejandro's gorgeous, but he's also…'

She faltered, glancing round at the pictures that covered Tamsin's walls, as if for inspiration. Mostly cut from the sports pages of newspapers and from old England rugby programmes, they showed Alejandro D'Arienzo's dark, brooding beauty from every angle. Serena shivered. Gorgeous certainly, but ruthless too.

'What, out of my league? You don't think this is going to

work, do you?' said Tamsin with an edge of despair. 'You don't think he's going to fancy me at all.'

Serena looked down into her sister's face. Tamsin's green eyes glowed as if lit by some internal sunlight and her cheeks were flushed with nervous excitement.

'That's not it at all. Of course he'll fancy you.' She sighed. 'And that's exactly what's bothering me.'

Above the majestic carved fireplace in the entrance hall of Harcourt Manor was a portrait of some seventeenth-century Calthorpe, smiling smugly against a backdrop of galleons on a stormy sea. Across the top, in flamboyantly embellished script, was written: *God blew and they were scattered.*

Alejandro D'Arienzo felt his face set in an expression of sardonic amusement as he looked into the cold, hooded eyes of Henry Calthorpe's forebear. There was no discernible resemblance between the two men, although they obviously shared a mutual hatred of the Spanish. Alejandro could just remember his father's stories, as a child in Argentina, of how their distant ancestors had been amongst the original *conquistadors* who had sailed from Spain to the New World. Those stories were one of the few tiny fragments of family identity that he had.

Moving restlessly away from the portrait, he ran a finger inside the stiff collar of his shirt and looked around at the impressive hallway, with its miles of intricate plasterwork ceiling and acres of polished wooden panelling. His team-mates stood in groups, laughing and drinking with dignitaries from the Rugby Football Union and the few sports journalists lucky enough to make the guest list, while the same assortment of blonde, well-bred rugby groupies circulated amongst them, flirting and flattering.

Henry Calthorpe, the England rugby coach, had made a big deal about holding the party to announce the new squad at his stunning ancestral home, claiming it showed that they were a team, a unit, a *family*. Remembering this now, Alejandro couldn't stop his lips curling into a sneer of savage, cynical amusement.

Everything about Harcourt Manor could have been specifically designed to emphasise exactly how much of an outsider Alejandro was. And he was damned sure that Henry Calthorpe had reckoned on that very thing.

At first Alejandro had thought he was being overly sensitive, that years in the English public school system had made him too quick to be on the defensive against bullying and victimization—but lately the coach's animosity had become too obvious to ignore. Alejandro was playing better than he'd ever done, too well to be dropped from the team without reason, but the fact was that Calthorpe wanted him out. He was just waiting for Alejandro to slip up.

Alejandro hoped Calthorpe was a patient man, because he had no intention of obliging. He was at the top of his game and he planned to stay there.

Draining the champagne in one go, he put the glass down on a particularly expensive-looking carved chest and glanced disdainfully around the room. There was not a single person he wanted to talk to, he thought wearily. The girls were identikit blondes with cut-glass accents and Riviera suntans, whose conversation ranged from clothes to the hilarious exploits of people they'd gone to school with, and whom they assumed Alejandro would know. Several times at parties like these he'd ended up sleeping with one just to shut her up.

But tonight it all seemed too much effort. The England tie felt like a noose around his neck, and suddenly he needed to be outside in the cool air, out of this suffocating atmosphere of complacency and privilege. Adrenalin pounded through him as he pushed his way impatiently through the groups of people towards the door.

And that was when he saw her.

She was standing in the doorway, her head lowered slightly, one hand gripping the doorframe for support, giving her an air of shyness and uncertainty that was totally at odds with her short black dress and very high heels. But he didn't notice the details of what she was wearing. It was her eyes that held him.

They were beautiful—green perhaps, almond shaped, slanting—but that was almost incidental. What made the breath catch in his throat was the laser-beam intensity of her gaze, which he could feel even from this distance.

His footsteps slowed as he got closer to her, but her gaze didn't waver. She straightened slightly, as if she had been waiting for him, and her hand fell from the doorframe and smoothed down her short skirt.

'You're not leaving?'

Her voice was so low and hesitant, and her words halfway between a question and a statement. He gave a twisted smile.

'I think it would be best if I did.'

He made to push past her. Close up, he could see that behind the smoky eye make up and the shiny inviting lip gloss she was younger than he'd at first thought. Her skin was clear and golden, and he noticed the frantic jump of the pulse in her throat. She was trembling slightly.

'No,' she said fiercely. 'Please. Don't leave.'

Interest flared up inside him, sudden and hot. He stopped, looking down at her sexy, rebellious dress, and then let his gaze move slowly back up to her face. Her cheeks were lightly stained with pink, and the eyes that looked up at him from under a fan of long, black lashes were dark and glittering. Seductive, but pleading.

'Why not?'

Lowering her chin, she kept them fixed on his, while she took his hand and stepped backwards, pulling him with her. Her hand felt small in his, and her touch sent a small shower of shooting stars up his arm.

'Because I want you.' She smiled shyly, dropping her gaze. 'I want you to stay.'

CHAPTER ONE

Six years later.

LEANING against the wall of the players' tunnel at Twickenham when the final whistle went was a bit like being trapped inside the body of a giant beast in pain. Tamsin hadn't been able to face watching the game, but she knew from the great, roaring groan that shook the ground beneath her feet and vibrated through her whole body that England had just fallen.

St George might have slain the dragon, but he'd certainly met his match in the mighty Barbarians.

Not that Tamsin was bothered about that. The team could have lost to a bunch of squealing six-year-old girls for all she cared, as long as they looked good while they were doing it.

She let out a shaky breath, pushing herself up and away from the wall, and discovering that her legs felt almost too weak to hold her up. This was the moment when she had to find out whether all the work of the past few months—and the frantic damage-limitation panic of the last eighteen hours—had paid off.

Like a sleepwalker she moved hesitantly to the mouth of the tunnel and looked out into the stadium, which stretched around her like some vast gladiatorial arena. Heads bent against the thin drizzle, shoulders stooped in defeat, the England team was making its way back towards the dressing room. Tamsin looked anxiously from one player to the next and, oblivious to the dejection and bewilderment on their exhausted faces, felt nothing but relief.

The players might not have performed brilliantly, but as far as she could see their shirts had, and to Tamsin—designer of the new and much-publicised England strip—that was all that mattered. She had already been on the receiving end of numerous barbed comments about what a coincidence it was that such a prestigious commission had been landed by the daughter of the new RFU chairman, so any whisper of failure on her part would be professional suicide.

Wearily, she dragged a hand through her short platinum-blonde hair and rubbed her tired eyes. *That was why it was kind of important that news of last night's little crisis with the pink shirts didn't get out.*

At the entrance to the tunnel, the bitter east wind that had made kicking so difficult for the players all afternoon almost knocked her over, slicing straight through her long ex-army greatcoat to the flimsy cocktail dress she wore beneath it. She'd left last night's charity fashion-gala early and gone straight to the factory, and hadn't had time to go home and change. Ten hours, numerous therapeutic phone-rants to Serena and a lot of very black coffee later, they'd had just enough newly printed shirts for the squad, but she'd spent the whole match praying there would be no sub-stitutions. Only now did she feel she could breathe more easily.

The feeling lasted all of ten seconds.

Then she felt her mouth open in wordless horror. Looking up at the huge screen at the top of the south stand, the air was squeezed from her lungs and replaced with something that felt like napalm.

It was *him*.

So that was why the England squad had lost.

Alejandro D'Arienzo was back. And this time he was playing for the opposition. Tamsin's heart seemed to have jumped out of her ribcage and lodged somewhere in her throat. How often in the last six years since that wonderful, devastating night at Harcourt had she thought she'd seen Alejandro D'Arienzo? Even though in her head she knew that he'd gone back to Argentina, how many times had she found herself turning round to look again at a tall, dark-haired man on a London street? Or felt her pulse start to race as she caught a glimpse of a sculpted profile through the tinted windows of a sportscar, only to experience a sickening thud of disappointment and simultaneous relief when she'd seen that it was some less charismatic stranger?

Now, staring up at the vast screen, she knew there was no such respite, and no mistaking that powerfully elegant body, the broad, muscular shoulders beneath the black-and-white Barbarians' shirt, and the arrogant tilt of that dark, dark head.

The crowd broke out in spontaneous applause as the TV cameras closed in on him, and the image of his beautiful, unsmiling face filled the screen, above the words *Man of the Match*. He was still wearing a gum shield which accentuated the sensual fullness of his contemptuous mouth—bloodied from the game—and the hollows beneath his high cheekbones. A red bandana held back his damp black hair, and for a second his restless, gold-flecked eyes glanced into the camera.

It felt like he was looking straight at her.

She wanted to take her eyes from the screen, but some in-built masochistic streak prevented her, and she was left staring helplessly up at him. Six years dissolved away and she was eighteen again, incandescent with fear and excitement as his eyes had met hers and he had walked across the hall at Harcourt towards her...

The England players had lined up on either side of the tunnel and were clapping the Barbarians in, but suddenly Ben Saunders, a young England player who'd been playing in the number-ten position for the first time, broke away and began to walk back across the field. Numbly Tamsin watched as he pulled his shirt over his head and held it out to Alejandro in a gesture of respect.

For a second the proud Argentinean didn't move. A tense hush seemed to fall over the stadium as the crowd watched. It was as if they were holding their breath, waiting to see whether Alejandro D'Arienzo, former England golden-boy, would accept the shirt he had played in with such glorious finesse before turning his back on the team so suddenly all those years ago.

The cameras zoomed in, but the sinister stillness of his face gave nothing away.

And then a huge roar of delight and excitement went up as Alejandro took hold of the hem of his own shirt and brought it slowly upwards over his head. Every hollow, every perfectly defined muscle beneath the bronze, sweat-sheened skin of his taut stomach filled the huge screens at both ends of the ground. And then, as he pulled the Barbarians shirt right off, the crowd screamed and whistled as they saw the tattoo of the sun—the symbol on the Argentine flag—right over his heart.

Vaguely aware that her chest hurt with the effort of breathing, and her fists were clenched so tightly that the fingernails were digging into her palms, Tamsin turned away with a snort of disgust.

Sure, Alejandro D'Arienzo was gorgeous. That was indisputable. But so was the fact that he was the coldest, most arrogant bastard who had ever breathed. It was just that most people hadn't been unlucky enough to see that side of him.

She had. And she still bore the scars. So why was she turning round again, and staring like some moon-struck adolescent as he walked back across the pitch, pulling on the white shirt? The crowd were on their feet, turning the stands into a rippling sea of red and white as they waved their flags joyously at seeing their unforgotten hero back in an England shirt.

And suddenly it hit her; the implication of what she had just witnessed finally penetrated her dazed brain.

An England shirt.

Alejandro D'Arienzo in an *England* shirt.

A precious, produced-at-the-last-minute, paid-for-in-blood-sweat-and-tears England shirt… One of the ones she absolutely couldn't afford to lose.

'*No!*'

With a horrified gasp, Tamsin leapt forward, her four-inch

heels sinking into the mud as she desperately tried to push her way through the crush of journalists, coaches, physios and groupies to reach the mouth of the tunnel before he did.

'Please, I have to…'

It was as if she was invisible. There were too many people, and the noise from the ecstatic crowd was too great. The moment he stepped from the pitch, journalists closed around Alejandro like iron filings around a magnet, and Tamsin was forced backwards by an impenetrable wall of bodies. Her heart was hammering, her body suddenly pulsing with heat beneath her heavy coat, and all thoughts but one had been driven from her shocked brain.

The shirt. She had to get the shirt back, or else…

With a whimper of horror, she tried again, taking advantage of her relative slightness to duck beneath the arm of a muscular ground official in a fluorescent jacket. Someone behind grabbed her coat and tried to pull her back, but panic gave her strength, and with a desperate lunge Tamsin broke free.

The England number two in front of her turned round and, recognising her, moved aside to let her through. At the same moment Alejandro finished talking to a journalist and stepped forwards.

There was hardly time to register what was happening, much less to stop it. Already unsteady on last night's killer heels, Tamsin felt herself hurtling forwards into open space, where she'd expected to encounter a solid and immovable row of muscular bodies, but just as she was falling strong arms seized her and she was lifted off her feet.

'Tamsin! Steady, darlin'.' It was Matt Fitzpatrick, the England number five. He grinned at her good-naturedly, revealing a missing front tooth. 'Don't tell me—when you saw my glorious try in the first half you finally realised you couldn't live without me?'

She shook her head. 'I'm…I need…' Her voice came out as a breathless croak, and she looked wildly around, just in time to see Alejandro disappearing into the tunnel. 'Him,' she said in a hoarse whisper.

Matt shrugged his shoulders and gave a theatrical sigh of

regret. 'I see. Can't argue with that, I suppose.' And with that he hoisted her into his muscular arms and pushed easily through the crowd before she could protest. 'D'Arienzo!'

Horror flooded her and she let out a squeal, which bounced off the walls of the tunnel. 'Matt, no!' she shrieked, wriggling frantically in his giant's arms, aware that her coat had fallen off her shoulders and the skirt of her tight black-satin cocktail dress was riding up to mid-thigh, showing the lacy tops of her stockings. But it was too late. As if in slow motion, she watched Alejandro stop.

Turn.

Look at her.

And then look away, without the slightest flicker of interest or recognition.

'Yes?'

He was talking to Matt, his eyebrows raised slightly.

'Someone wants you,' grinned Matt, setting her down on her feet. Tamsin ducked her head. Her blood felt like it had been diluted with five parts of vodka as misery churned inside her, mixing uneasily with wild relief. He didn't recognise her. Of course he didn't—her hair had been darker then, and longer. She'd been younger.

And she'd meant absolutely nothing to him.

It was fine. It was good. The humiliation of facing him again if he'd remembered that night would have been terminally appalling. Some in-built instinct for self-preservation told her not to look up, not to meet the eyes of the man who had blown her world to smithereens and walked away without a scratch, to keep her head down.

Oh, God. Her self-preservation instinct hadn't reckoned on the effect of looking at the length of his bare, muscular thighs.

'Really?' he said in a quiet, steel-edged voice. 'And what could Lady Tamsin Calthorpe possibly want with me?'

Adrenalin scorched through her like wildfire, and she felt her head jerk backwards. Towering above her, he was smiling slightly, but the expression in his eyes was as cold and bleak as the North Sea.

She raised her chin and forced herself to meet his gaze. So he *did* remember. And he had the nerve to look at her as if she was the one who had done something wrong. *Like what, for example—not being attractive enough?* Pressing her lips together, she pushed back the questions she had asked herself a million times since that awful night at Harcourt and simply said, 'Not you. The shirt. Could you take it off, please?'

Looking up into his face was like torment. She should have been used to it—she'd seen it in her dreams often enough in the last six years—but even the most vivid of them hadn't done justice to the brutal beauty of him as he stood only a foot away. Bruised and bloodied, he was every inch the conquering Barbarian.

'Oh, dear,' he drawled. 'What's it been—five years? And clearly nothing's changed.'

Oh, Lord; his voice. The melodic Spanish lilt that he'd all but lost growing up in England was stronger again now. Unfortunately.

Tamsin swallowed. 'Six,' she snapped, and instantly wanted to bite out her tongue for giving him the satisfaction of knowing that she cared enough to remember. 'Anyway, I don't know what you mean. From where I'm standing, plenty has changed.'

Like I'm not naïve enough any more to think that the face of an angel and the body of a living god make a shallow, callous bastard into a hero. She didn't say the words, but just thinking them, and remembering what he'd done, made the strength seep back into her trembling body.

'Really?' He nodded slowly, reaching out a strong, tanned hand and smoothing it over the wing of pale-gold hair that fell over one eye. 'Well, there's this, of course, but I'm not talking about superficial things. It's what's underneath that I'm more interested in.' Guilty, humiliating heat flared in the pit of her stomach as his gaze flickered over her, taking in the black-satin cocktail dress beneath the huge overcoat, and the muddied sky-scraper shoes that clearly said she hadn't been home last night.

'I'm sure that line about taking the shirt off usually enjoys a very high success rate, especially since your daddy is now so high up in the RFU, but that cuts absolutely no ice with me these days. I'm out of all that—' He broke off, and laughed. 'Though, of course, I don't have to tell you that, do I?'

She would not melt. She would not succumb to his voice or his touch, or his questions, or anything. Looking over his right shoulder at the red cross of St George painted on the wall of the tunnel, she affected a tone of deep boredom.

'Whatever. I just want the shirt back, please.'

Wordlessly, as if he were weighing up what to do next, Alejandro took a step towards her, closing the gap between them. The other players were filing past them and the tunnel echoed with their shouts and the clatter of their studs on the floor, but the noise seemed to be coming from miles away. Tamsin felt her flimsy façade slipping. The physical reality of his closeness was acting on her senses like a drug, giving her a painfully height-ened awareness of his broad, sculpted chest beneath the tightly fitting shirt, the scent of damp grass and mud that clung to him, and its undertone of raw masculinity.

'I'm sure you do,' he said thoughtfully. 'I'm sure the last thing your father wants is to see me back in an England shirt. After all, he tried hard enough to get me out of one six years ago.'

'Yes, well, you have to agree that the Barbarians strip is much more appropriate, Alejandro. Given that you behave like one.'

A lazy smile pulled the corners of his sexy, swollen mouth. With a nonchalant lift of his shoulders, he turned and began to walk away from her, his massive shoulders filling the narrow space. He called the shots here, and he knew it.

'Wait!'

Fury welled inside her and she ran after him, suddenly finding that without the distraction of his closeness she could think clearly again, and fuelled by a renewed sense of urgency to reclaim the shirt. Slipping past him, she placed herself defiantly in the doorway of the visitors' changing room, blocking his way.

'The shirt, Alejandro.'

She saw the dangerous gleam in the depths of his tiger's eyes, and for a split second wondered if he was going to push her out of the way. Given the relative size of them, he'd hardly have to try, but something in him seemed to prevent him. If she didn't know any better she'd think it was some sense of inherent chivalry, but that would be ridiculous, because she knew better than anyone that there wasn't an atom of decency in the whole of Alejandro D'Arienzo's magnificent body.

He stood back, raising both his hands as if in surrender, but his face bore a look of subdued triumph.

'OK—go on, then. Take it.'

She cast a furtive look around. The tunnel was emptier now, but there were still officials, a few cameramen and journalists hovering outside the press room. '*Me?* Take it off *you?* Don't be ridiculous. I can't.

Alejandro gave a small shrug and dropped his hands. 'I think we both know that you can, because you've done it before. But if you don't *want* to…' He came towards her and she found herself automatically stepping aside. 'Obviously it's not that important.'

'It is.'

She spoke through gritted teeth, trying to keep back the scream of frustration and fury that was gathering in her chest. Alejandro's hand was on the door and she reached out and grabbed his arm.

It was as if she'd touched a bolt of lightning. White-hot tongues of electricity sizzled up her arm and exploded inside her, simply from the contact of his body beneath the shirt. How come in six years this had never happened with anyone else, even when she'd wanted it to?

He stopped, then slowly turned round so he was standing with his back against the door. 'OK, then. If it matters so much, you'd better take it.'

He was challenging her, she realised, and Tamsin Calthorpe was a girl who could never resist a challenge. Her eyes were pinned to his as she moved towards him, her heart pounding painfully in her chest. *Just do it*, she thought wildly. *You're a big girl now, not that gauche and gullible teenager. Show him that he can't intimidate you…*

She made a short exhalation of exasperation and disgust. Quickly, so he couldn't see how much her hands were shaking, she took hold of the hem of the shirt and tugged it roughly upwards, while he stood unhelpfully motionless, his gaze fixed mockingly on her face.

'You're enjoying this, aren't you?' she hissed.

'Being undressed so tenderly by a beautiful woman?' he drawled with heavy irony. 'Who wouldn't?'

Viciously she yanked his arms up, standing on her tiptoes to pull the shirt over them, her breath coming in uneven gasps with the effort of manhandling his immensely powerful body, and of hiding the screaming, treacherous desire that it aroused in her. But as she reached up he made a sudden, sharp move backwards so that the door swung open and she fell against his chest with a cry of anguish and surprise.

A raucous cheer and a volley of wolf-whistles rang around the Barbarians' dressing room. Tamsin froze in horror, her hands still entangled in the rugby shirt which was now midway over Alejandro's chest, realising exactly how it must look.

Exactly how Alejandro had intended it to look.

'Don't tell me you're not enjoying it too,' he murmured. The amusement in his voice was unmistakable.

As she disengaged herself and stepped back, Tamsin felt an eerie calm descend on her. It was as if, in those few seconds, she was selecting an emotion from a range displayed before her: the murderous rage was tempting, or the cathartic, hysterical indignation… But, no. It might be difficult to carry off, but she was going to go for something a little more sophisticated.

She felt her mouth curve into a languid, slightly patronising smile as she took the bottom of the shirt gingerly between her finger and thumb, and pulled it disdainfully down, covering up the sinuous convex sweep of Alejandro's stomach.

'Cover yourself up, D'Arienzo,' she said scathingly. 'When I said "nice strip" I was referring to the shirt.'

The changing room erupted in whoops and whistles of appreciation as Tamsin turned on her heel and, casting a last, pitying glance at Alejandro, swept out. Her rush of triumph and elation lasted just long enough for the door to slam behind her, and then she collapsed, shaking, against the wall.

Suddenly the shirt seemed like the least of her problems.

Ignoring the boisterous cheers of his team-mates, Alejandro pulled off the shirt and tossed it contemptuously down on the bench before grabbing a towel and heading grimly towards the bathroom beyond the changing area. He felt none of the physical exhaustion that usually descended on him in the immediate aftermath of a game. Thanks to that close encounter with the High Priestess of Seduction and Betrayal, his mind was racing, his body still pulsing with adrenalin.

Adrenalin and other more inconvenient hormones.

The bathroom was a spartan white-tiled room with six huge claw-footed baths arranged facing each other in two rows, each filled with iced water. Research showed that an ice bath immediately after a game minimised the impact of injury, and shocked the body into a quicker recovery, but this didn't make the practice any more popular with players. In the nearest tub the blond Australian giant, Dean Randall, sat still in full kit, grim-faced and shivering with cold. He glanced up as Alejandro came in.

'Welcome to the Twickenham spa, mate,' he joked weakly through chattering teeth. 'I'd have kept that shirt on if I were you. It doesn't make much difference, but, by God, anything's better than nothing.'

Alejandro didn't flinch as he stepped into the bath.

'I think I'll take my chances with the cold rather than wear an England shirt for any longer than necessary,' he said brutally, closing his eyes briefly as the icy water tore into him like the teeth of some savage animal. For a second his body screamed with exquisite agony before numbness took hold, mercifully obliterating the insistent pulse of desire that had been reverberating through him since Tamsin had tried to strip the shirt from him.

Randall forced a laugh. 'No plans to come back, then?'

'No.' Alejandro's gritted teeth had nothing to do with the freezing water. 'It would take a whole lot more than a fancy new strip to make me come back and play for England.'

Like an apology from Henry Calthorpe. And his daughter.

Randall nodded. 'You came to settle old scores?'

'Nothing so dramatic,' said Alejandro tersely. 'It's business. I'm one of the sponsors of the Argentine rugby team.'

'Los Pumas?' Randall gave a low, shaky whistle of respect and Alejandro smiled bleakly. 'I'm here because, with another World Cup looming, it's time everyone was reminded that Argentina are major contenders.'

'I wish I could argue with that, mate.' At the physio's nod the huge Australian stood up and vaulted over the side of the bath, wrapping his arms around his body and jumping from foot to foot to bring the circulation back to his frozen legs. 'You certainly showed them today, at any rate. They'd have walked all over us if it hadn't been for you. I owe you a drink at the party tonight. You'll be there?'

Alejandro nodded. Just thinking about the last England team party he'd attended made the agony of the iced water fade into insignificance. He frowned, resting his elbows on the sides of the bath, and bringing his clenched fists up to his temples as unwelcome memories of that night came flooding back: the damp, earthy smell of the conservatory at Harcourt and the warm scent of her hair, the velvety feel of her skin beneath his shaking fingers as he'd undone the laced bodice of her dress.

'OK, Alejandro, time's up,' said the physio.

Alejandro didn't move. A muscle hammered in his cheek as he remembered pulling away from her, struggling to fight back the rampaging lust she had unleashed in him long enough to find someone to lend him a condom. Telling her he wouldn't be long, he had rushed out into the corridor…and straight into Henry Calthorpe.

The expression of murderous rage on his face had told Alejandro instantly who the girl in the conservatory was. And exactly what it would mean to his career. In one swift, devastatingly masochistic stroke, Alejandro had handed Henry Calthorpe the justification he'd been looking for. An excuse so perfect…

'You some kind of masochist, D'Arienzo? I said, time's up.'

An excuse so perfect it was impossible to believe it had happened by chance. Alejandro stood up, letting the iced water cascade down his numb body for a second before stepping out of the bath. That explained the directness of her approach. He'd thought there was something honest about her, something refreshingly open, but in fact it had been exactly the opposite.

She had deliberately set him up.

Back in the dressing room, he picked up the discarded England shirt and looked at it as he brutally rubbed the feeling back into his frozen limbs. The new design was visually arresting and technologically ground-breaking, and, in spite of himself, he was grudgingly impressed. Impressed and intrigued. Applying similar design principles and fabric technology to his polo-team kit would make playing in the heat of the Argentinean summer he had just left behind so much more bearable. Thoughtfully he picked it up and was just about to put it into his kit-bag when his eye was caught by the number on the back.

Number ten.

It all came crashing back. For a moment he'd allowed himself to forget that this was so much more than just a cleverly designed piece of sports kit. This shirt, the England number ten, was what he had spent so many miserable, lonely years striving for. When it had felt like there was nothing else to live for, this had been his goal, his destiny, his holy grail, and through his own hard work, his own blood and sweat, he'd achieved it.

Only to have had it snatched away from him, thanks to Tamsin Calthorpe.

In one swift, savage movement he threw the shirt into his bag and swore viciously. So she wanted this back, did she? Well, it would be interesting to see how far she would go to get it this time, because Alejandro didn't intend to relinquish it easily.

Tamsin Calthorpe had been directly and knowingly responsible for him being stripped of his England shirt six years ago. She owed him this.

And a lot more besides.

CHAPTER TWO

'HUMILIATING doesn't even begin to describe it,' Tamsin moaned, clutching the phone and sinking down into the steaming bath-water. 'I mean, it would have been bad enough if he hadn't remembered me, but it was a million times worse when he did...'

Sticking a foot out of the water, she used it to turn on the hot tap with a dexterity born of long practice and added, 'Obviously I can't go to the party now.'

'Don't be silly,' said Serena mildly. 'You've got to. You can't let him get to you like that.'

'I've got a splitting headache, anyway,' Tamsin said sulkily. 'It's probably the start of a really bad migraine.'

'You don't get migraines.'

'Yes, well, there's always a first time. Look, Serena, it's all very well to say I shouldn't let him get to me, but it's a bit late for that, wouldn't you agree? It's not just about what happened today; it's about the fact that Alejandro D'Arienzo got to me six years ago and completely—'

'Exactly. Six years.' Her sister's calm logic was beginning to wind Tamsin up. 'You were a teenager, for goodness' sake—we all make mistakes and do things we regret when we're young.'

'You didn't,' Tamsin snapped, making islands of bubbles on the surface of the water. 'You played it so cool that Simon was virtually on his knees with a ring before you'd kissed him. I, on the other hand, was so deranged with infatuation for Alejandro that I dressed like I was charging for it and didn't even take the time to tell him my name before I threw myself at him.'

'So? It's in the past. Like I said, we make mistakes, and we *move on.*'

'I know, but…' Tamsin knew Serena was right. In theory. 'Moving on' sounded so simple and logical. So why had she never been able to do it? Even Serena had no idea of the extent to which what had happened that night had affected her in the years that followed. And was still affecting her now. 'I can't.'

'I'm sorry, I'm going to have to stop you right there. I thought tonight was about your work not our sex life.' *Ouch.* 'I thought that you were going to the party to unveil the England team suits?' Serena gave a breezy laugh. 'Gosh, just think: all those people who said you were flaky and you only got the commission because of Dad will *love* it if you don't turn up because of some bloke!'

Tamsin stood up in a rush of water.

'*What?* Who said that?'

'Oh, well, no one in particular,' soothed Serena. 'Not in so many words, anyway, although Simon said that article in last week's *Sports Journal* sort of implied—'

'God, I *hate* that!' Snatching a towel, Tamsin stepped out of the bath and stormed into the bedroom, stepping over the chaos of discarded clothes and piles of magazines, and leaving a trail of wet footprints on her polished wooden floorboards. 'How *dare* they say that? Don't they do their research? Don't they know I have a first-class degree in textiles, and that I was up against some of the stiffest competition in the business to get this commission? Don't they know that Coronet won "best new label" at last year's British Fashion Awards?'

'I'm not sure, but *I* do,' said Serena placidly. 'It's the press pack at the party that you need to be haranguing, not me. Although, of course, if you're not there I don't suppose you can. You'll just have to let the clothes speak for themselves. The suits are exquisite, and from what I gathered from Simon the new shirts were very—'

Tamsin, who had flung herself down on top of the mountain of clothes piled on her un-made bed, gave a cry of dismay and slithered to her feet. 'Oh, my God, the *shirt*! I'd almost forgotten about that. I have to get it back. If I don't, by the end of tomorrow's press conference my reputation is going to be toast, and on top of everything else that's the last thing I need.'

'How are things at Coronet?' asked Serena carefully.

'Bad. While I was dealing with the shirt crisis, Sally left a message on my answerphone to say that another buyer had pulled out because of loss of exclusivity, since the designs have been so widely copied on the high street.'

'Imitation is the sincerest form of flattery, darling,' Serena said weakly. 'And the shirt crisis wasn't your fault. The factory messed up the dye process, and it's entirely to your credit that you thought to test the shirts for colour-fastness ahead of the game.' Serena giggled. 'Otherwise England would have been playing in pink by half time.'

'Given that the press are out for my blood already, I don't think they'll see it that way.' Tamsin threw open her wardrobe and began to rifle through the rails. 'Which is why I can't afford for it to get out.'

'What's that noise? What are you doing?'

'Looking for something to wear.'

'Ah. Does that mean you're going?'

'Oh yes, I'm going all right,' Tamsin said grimly, pulling out a sea-green silk dress, grimacing and putting it back. 'I'm fed up of being taken advantage of. Alejandro bloody D'Arienzo picked the wrong day to mess with me. He screwed me up enough last time, and I'm not going to give him the satisfaction of doing it again. He took something that belongs to me.' She paused, frowning. 'And I intend to take it back.'

'Are we talking about the England shirt now?' said Serena gently.

'Amongst other things.' *Let's see: my pride, my sense of worth, my self-confidence…* 'God, Serena, when I think about that night—about how it felt when I realised he wasn't coming back… I thought nothing could be worse than knowing that he found me so unattractive back then, but you should have seen the expression on his face this afternoon. It's like he *hates* me, like he has nothing but contempt for me. Like I'm *worthless*.'

'Don't say that, Tam.' Serena's voice hardened slightly. 'He was the one in the wrong back then. You're brilliant. And beautiful.'

Tamsin stopped, catching sight of herself suddenly in the wardrobe mirror. Wrapped only in a towel, her newly washed hair was slicked back from a face that was flushed from the bath. So far, so OK, but her eyes automatically travelled downwards to her right arm.

She grimaced and turned away.

'Yeah, right. And you're clearly suffering from pregnancy hormones,' Tamsin said with a rueful grin. 'Go and eat another pickled onion and chocolate-spread sandwich and leave me alone. Don't you know I have a party to get ready for?'

'Not so fast. I need to know what you're wearing first. You can keep your weird sandwich combinations; now that I know I'm condemned to spending the next six months in a maternity smock, my only craving is for tailored clothes, so I'll have to indulge myself through you. You need something that screams *"successful, glamorous, assured, mysterious, sexy, but completely unavailable"*.'

Tamsin pulled out a narrow slither of light-as-air ash-grey chiffon and looked at it thoughtfully. 'Exactly.'

'You look lovely, darling,' Henry Calthorpe said stiffly, barely glancing up from the evening paper in his hand as Tamsin slid into the back of the car beside him. 'Nice dress.'

'Thank you, Daddy.'

Tamsin suppressed a smile. She was grateful for the sentiment—sort of—but it would be great if for once he'd actually looked. Then he would have seen that the dress wasn't *nice*—it was a triumph. It was her favourite design for the new season's collection; the whisper-fine chiffon was generously gathered from a low V-neck, crisscrossed by bands of silver ribbon which fitted snugly under the bust and swept downwards at the back, giving the whole thing a slightly Greek feel. The long semi-sheer sleeves fell down over her hands, covering her arms. Of course; fashion wasn't her father's thing, but he certainly would have noticed if she'd left her arms bare.

'Initial comment on the strip seems to be fairly positive, you'll be pleased to know,' Henry continued acidly. 'It's just a shame they didn't manage to get a picture of one of our players wearing it.'

He closed the paper and put it down quickly, but not before Tamsin had caught a glimpse of a full-page photograph of Alejandro walking from the pitch in the England shirt beneath the headline: *Barbarian Conqueror*.

She picked up the newspaper and opened it. In the hushed interior of the Mercedes, her heart was beating so loudly she was surprised her father couldn't hear it. Trying to keep her hand from shaking as she held the paper, she began to read.

> *Former England hero Alejandro D'Arienzo made a welcome return to Twickenham this afternoon in a closely fought match between England and the Barbarians. In a stunning display of skill, the Argentine Adonis helped the Barbarians to a surprise 36-32 victory, after which an outclassed Ben Saunders handed D'Arienzo his new shirt in a gesture of well-deserved respect.*
>
> *The crowd were clearly delighted to see D'Arienzo back in the England number ten shirt, the position he famously made his own in his three years in the England squad. His international career came to an abrupt and mysterious end six years ago amid rumours of a personality clash with then-coach Sir Henry Calthorpe, and D'Arienzo returned to his homeland where he has earned a formidable reputation in the polo world, as both patron and player for the high-goal San Silvana team.*

Both sides have always maintained a steely silence on events that led to this defection, but his dazzling performance today, coupled with reports that he is closely involved with Los Pumas, must make Calthorpe wonder if he would have been better swallowing his pride and keeping him on...

'Utter rubbish,' said Henry tartly as Tamsin folded the paper with exaggerated care and put it down on the seat between them.

Picking idly at a bead on the sleeve of her dress, Tamsin kept her voice neutral as she said, 'You never liked him, though, did you?'

Henry suddenly seemed hugely interested in the featureless black landscape beyond the car window. 'I didn't trust him,' he said with quiet bitterness. Then, turning back to Tamsin, he gave a bland smile. 'He was dangerous. A loose cannon. No loyalty to the team with that...that God-awful tattoo on his chest. The press conveniently forget all that now, don't they?'

Tamsin felt the breath catch painfully in her throat as the image of Alejandro's chest, with the Argentine sun blazing on the hard plane of muscle over his heart, filled her head. As a teenager she had cut a picture from a magazine that had showed him stripped to the waist during one hot summer training session for the World Cup. Even now, all these years later, she could still recall the sensation of terrible, churning longing she'd felt whenever she looked at that tattoo.

The car slowed, and a scattering of flashbulbs from the other side of the darkened glass told her they'd arrived at the very exclusive hotel where the post-match party was being held. Tamsin blinked, dragging in a shaky breath and forcing herself back into the present as the car glided smoothly down the drive towards a solid-looking, square stone house half-covered with glossy creeper.

Even before the driver had opened the car door, the noise of the party was already clearly audible.

'After this afternoon's shameful performance, heaven knows

what they think they've got to celebrate,' said Henry cuttingly, getting out of the car. 'You'd better do the photo-call straight away while there's still some hope of the team doing justice to your elegant suits. If you leave it any later, they'll all be rolling drunk and singing obscene songs. Come on.'

Henry held out his arm. Absently, she took it. 'Oh, dear, you're right. And, since the photographer wants all those cheesy and predictable shots of the team holding me up like a rugby ball, I'd rather I was in sober hands.'

Instantly she felt Henry bristle. He stopped, and Tamsin instantly cursed herself for walking right into that one. It was all Alejandro D'Arienzo's fault. She wasn't thinking clearly, otherwise she would have been all too aware that her father's legendary and highly annoying protective streak was about to reveal itself. 'That's ridiculous,' he snapped. 'I'm not having my daughter mauled around by the entire team like some Playboy bunny. I'll have a word with the photographer and make it perfectly clear that—'

'No! Don't you dare! I got this commission on my own merit, and I'll handle the PR on my own terms.'

For a second they glared at each other in the light of the carriage lamps on either side of the front door. Then Henry withdrew his arm from hers and walked stiffly up the stone steps into the brightly lit reception hall, the set of his very straight back conveying his utter disapproval. Left alone outside, Tamsin gritted her teeth and stamped her foot.

Hell, he was *impossible*. It was all right for Serena; she'd always been able to wrap Henry round her little finger with a flash of her dimples and a flutter of her big blue eyes. Whereas Tamsin had always argued, and—

She paused.

Then, running quickly up the steps in her father's wake, she caught up with him in the centre of the panelled reception area.

'Please, Daddy.' She caught hold of his arm, forcing him to stop. Picturing Serena's lovely face in her mind's eye, and trying desperately to assume the same gentle, beseeching expression, Tamsin looked up at her father. 'It's only a couple of photographs,' she said persuasively.

It worked like a charm. Instantly she saw the slight softening in Henry's chilly grey gaze, and he nodded almost imperceptibly. 'All right,' he said gruffly. 'You know best. I'll let you get on with it.'

Relief flooded her, and impulsively she reached up to kiss his cheek. 'Thank you, Daddy.'

Turning, she ran lightly across the hallway, just about managing to resist punching the air, but unable to stop a most un-Serenalike smile of elation breaking across her face.

Alejandro froze at the top of the stairs, his face as cold and impassive as the rows of portraits on the oak-panelled walls around him as he took in the touching little scene below.

He saw her cross the hallway in a ripple of silvery grey chiffon, her pale hair gleaming in the light from the chandelier above. He watched her tilt her face up to her father, looking up at him from under her dark lashes, and heard the persuasive, pleading tone in her husky voice as she spoke.

Please, Daddy... Thank you, Daddy... It was as much as he could do not to laugh out loud at the saccharine sweetness in her voice, but a second later his sardonic amusement evaporated as she turned away, and the melting look on her face gave way to a smile of pure triumph.

The calculating bitch.

Nothing had changed, he thought bitterly, carrying on down the corridor to his room. Not deep down, anyway. She'd cut her hair and gone blonde big style, but the glittering green eyes, the attitude and the rich-girl arrogance were still the same.

Back in his room he checked his watch and picked up the phone. It was just after five p.m. in Argentina, and the grooms would be turning the ponies out for the night. Two promising mares—a chestnut, and a pretty palomino that he'd bought last month in America for the new polo season—had been delivered yesterday and he was impatient to hear how they were settling in.

Giselle, his PA back at San Silvana, reassured him that the horses were doing fine. They'd recovered well from the journey, and the vet was happy that they would both be rested and ready to use on his return.

Alejandro felt better once he'd spoken to her. Nothing to do with the husky warmth in her voice, but simply because it was good to be reminded that San Silvana, with its rolling lawns, its stables, poolhouse and acres of lush paddock filled with ponies, was still there. Was real. Was his.

Coming back to England had dredged up insecurities he had long forgotten, he thought wryly, catching a glimpse of his reflection in the mirror as he went to the door. He'd come a long way, but beneath the bespoke dinner suit, the Savile Row shirt and silk bow-tie, there apparently still lurked the displaced boy who didn't belong.

Out on the galleried landing the sounds of the party drifted up to him. Glancing down on his way to the stairs, he could see the England players, standing shoulder to shoulder in identical dark suits as they lined up for a photograph. They had their backs to him, and were standing in two rows while a photographer wearing tight leather-trousers and an expression of extreme harassment tried to get them all to stop messing around and keep still.

'Fifty quid to swap places with Matt Fitzpatrick!' someone called from the back row, and there was a huge guffaw of laughter, followed by someone else shouting, 'A hundred!'

'Sensible offers only, please, gentlemen,' grinned Fitzpatrick.

For a second Alejandro didn't understand the joke, but then he moved further along the shadowed gallery and looked down, feeling his sore shoulders stiffen and ice-cold disgust flood him.

Tamsin Calthorpe, her cheeks glowing and her honeyed hair shining like the sun beneath the photographer's lights, was stretched out horizontally in the arms of the front row of players, facing out towards the camera. Matt Fitzpatrick, exuding

Neanderthal pride, supported her body, one huge hand cupped around her left breast.

The photographer's flash exploded as he took a volley of shots. Her bare legs and feet, held in the meaty hands of one of the England forwards, looked as delicate as the stem of some exotic flower, and next to the coarse, battered faces of the players Tamsin's skin gleamed like pale-gold satin.

'How come you get the best position anyway, Fitzpatrick?' shouted one of the younger players at the back.

Tamsin laughed, and to Alejandro the sound was like finger-nails on a blackboard. 'He's more experienced than you, Jones. And his handling skills are better.' As Jones blushed to the roots of his hair, the team erupted into more rowdy laughter and cheers.

So that was what she'd been asking her father for: permission to appear in the team photo. He remembered her soft, pleading tone as she'd put her hand on his arm and said 'only a couple of photographs'.

Had she no pride at all? Alejandro's face felt stiff with contempt as he leaned against one of the gallery's carved wooden posts and watched. What was she, some kind of unofficial team mascot? It was perfectly clear that she knew all the players pretty well.

How many had she slept with?

The thought slipped into his head without warning, but he had to brace himself against the lash of unexpected bitterness that accompanied it.

There was much clapping and shouting below as two of the players, under direction from the photographer, lifted her onto their shoulders. Laughing, Tamsin tipped back her head and looked up.

He watched the smile die on her glossy lips as her eyes met his.

In that moment Alejandro realised who it was she reminded him of: the blondes who'd populated the rugby parties he used to attend. The girl he'd thought was so different had grown up into one of those women he'd so despised at the party at Harcourt.

A polished, hard-society blonde whose satiny skin concealed a ruthless streak a mile wide. A professional flirt, a consummate party girl, a shallow, manipulative man-user whose every flattering word was meaningless and every smile was a lie.

And, judging from the look on her face now, she was all too aware she'd been found out.

No.

No, no no.

It couldn't be possible. Even her luck wasn't that bad. As the two props set her back on her feet, Tamsin shook her fringe from her eyes and looked back up into the minstrels' gallery where a figure in the shadows had caught her eye. A figure she'd thought for one nasty moment was…

Oh, God. It was. *Him.*

He was leaning insolently against a carved wooden post, looking down. Though his face was in shadow, every line of his elegant, powerful body seemed to communicate contemptuous amusement, and she could feel his eyes searing her with their intensity and their disdain.

The photographer clapped his hands and trilled, 'OK, people—are we ready? Now, if the two guys on either side of Miss Calthorpe could look down at her, please?'

Why? Why couldn't he just go?

Dimly Tamsin was aware of laughing banter breaking out around her again, and of Matt pulling her towards him and making some joking comment to the player on her other side. But, as she looked up into Matt's appreciative blue eyes, it was Alejandro's cold, contemptuous stare that she saw.

The photographer's flash exploded in her face as fury erupted inside her.

That was what he'd done to her *that* night.

'That's fabulous,' gushed the photographer. 'Really fabulous. Gorgeous, sexy pout, Miss Calthorpe. Now, shoulders straighter, Matt… Lovely.'

He'd broken something inside her, so that no matter how much men like Matt flattered her and flirted with her...

'Tamsin, you're looking *de*licious. Just put your hand on Matt's chest...yes, like that...'

...she could never quite make herself believe that they meant it.

'Now, let's make sure we get the nice rose-patterned lining of the jacket in the shot. Just slip your hand underneath his jacket, and sort of half-push it off his shoulder. Yeah, like that. That's gorgeous.'

Maybe it was time she proved to Alejandro Arrogant D'Arienzo, and herself, that not all men found her such a turn-off?

The shutter rattled like machine-gun fire. High on adrenalin, fuelled by fury, Tamsin let instinct take over. For six years she had surrounded herself with a forest of thorns, keeping men at bay with her endless succession of barbed comments and razor-sharp retorts, all because he had robbed her of the belief that she was desirable. But she would show him that she was attractive, she was sexy... Her spine arched reflexively as she slid her hand over Matt's shoulder, but it wasn't Matt she was thinking of. Turning her head towards the bright lights and the camera, lifting her chin in silent, brazen challenge, she looked into the shadows, straight into Alejandro's eyes.

It was like a steel trap closing around her—cold, hard, unyielding. He was looking down at her, the lights from below accentuating the sharp planes of his face, which were wholly at odds with the sensual swell of his mouth. And then, as she watched, he shook his head in an attitude of incredulous, pitying amusement.

He turned and walked away. Just as he had six years ago. He walked away, without a backwards glance, leaving the hot throb of desire ebbing from her and nothing but icy desolation and humiliation in its place.

CHAPTER THREE

BLUE ball, top-left pocket.

With narrowed eyes Alejandro looked thoughtfully at the billiard table. It was a difficult shot, and in his own personal game of dare this was sudden death.

If he got it in, he would play on. If he missed, he had to go back out and rejoin the party. He had to go out there and watch Tamsin Calthorpe tease and flirt her way around the rest of the England team. And, he thought with a grimace of scorn, judging by her earlier performance, probably most of the Barbarians as well.

It was probably just as well he never missed.

Lazily he bent to line up the shot. From the other side of the massive polished-wood door he could hear the raucous sounds of the party. As a major investor in Argentine rugby he ought to be out there; after today's game he was the man everyone wanted to talk to and he should be capitalising on that to get publicity for Los Pumas. That was, after all, what he'd come back for.

Unhurriedly he adjusted the balance of the cue. To even up the odds a little he closed his left eye, leaving only the bruised and swollen right one to judge the angle of the shot.

With a sharp, insouciant jab the blue fell neatly into the top-left pocket.

Alejandro straightened up, smiling ruefully as a sting of perverse disappointment sliced through him. He had no desire to go out there and mix with the great and the good of the rugby world, but there was a part of him that would have rather enjoyed the chance to watch the amazing Lady Calthorpe in operation some more, for no other reason than to marvel at how much more polished the routine had become in the last six years. Back then there had been a gawky awkwardness about her, a trembling sort of defiance, but it had affected him far more powerfully than tonight's virtuoso display of sexual invitation.

Powerful enough to cloud his judgement and get beneath his defences, he thought acidly.

She'd upped her game considerably since then, and as a result it seemed that she was no longer kept in the background as a handmaid for her father's sordid, secret schemes. Now she was much higher profile, which of course made perfect sense. Henry Calthorpe was now chairman of the RFU, and, judging by the photoshoot Alejandro had just witnessed, the organisation had become one big, indulgent playground for his spoiled daughter. He wondered how far her influence spread now.

With sudden violence he threw down the cue and went to stand in front of the fire.

Henry Calthorpe was obviously too important these days to invite the riff-raff into his own home, but the hotel had apparently been chosen to provide a very similar setting. The billiard room was a gentleman's retreat in typical English country-house style, with leather wing-backed chairs and oil paintings of hunting scenes on the walls. The long, fringed lamp hanging low over the table made the billiard balls glow like jewels in a pool of emerald green, and firelight glinted on a tray of cut-glass decanters beside him.

He reached for one and splashed a generous measure into a crystal tumbler, and had just thrown himself into one of the high-backed chairs facing the fire when there was a sudden rush of noise behind him as the door opened and then closed again quickly. Alejandro didn't move, but his hand tightened around the glass as, reflected in the mirror above the fireplace, he saw her.

She went straight to the billiard table and leaned against it, dropping her head and breathing hard, as if she was trying to steady herself or regain control. His first thought was that she was waiting for someone to follow her into the room, and he glanced towards the door again. But it stayed shut, and a moment later Tamsin Calthorpe lifted her head and he saw that the laboured breathing, the bright spots of colour on her cheeks, weren't caused by desire but by anger.

Picking up the cue he had so recently thrown down, she barely glanced at the table before stooping, and, with a snarl of fury, took a vicious shot which sent the balls cannoning wildly across the table.

In the mirror Alejandro watched the white rebound off the top cushion, just missing the pink and the black and sending the brown ball cannoning into the middle pocket. Still completely oblivious to his presence, Tamsin punched the air and gave a low hiss of triumph.

'Lucky shot,' he said sardonically.

In the mirror he saw her freeze, the billiard cue held across her body like a weapon.

'Who said luck had anything to do with it?'

Her voice was cool and haughty, but he caught the nervous dart of her eyes as she looked around to see who had spoken. Her blonde head was held high, her shoulders tense and alert. She looked oddly vulnerable, like a startled deer.

'It was a difficult one.' Alejandro stood up and turned slowly towards her, feeling a flicker of satisfaction as he watched her eyes widen in shock and the colour leave her face. She recovered quickly, shrugging as she walked towards the curtained windows.

'Precisely. What would have been the point in taking it if it was easy?'

It was Alejandro's turn to be stunned. As she walked away from him he saw that the dress that had looked so demure from the front was completely backless, showing a downwards sweep of flawless, peachy skin.

He made a sharp, scornful sound—halfway between a laugh and a sneer, which sent a tide of heat flooding into Tamsin's face and a torrent of boiling fury erupting inside her. Her heart was beating very hard as she whipped round to face him again.

'You don't believe me?'

'Frankly, no.' He moved around the chair and came towards her. He'd taken off his dinner jacket and undone the top two buttons of his shirt. His silk bow-tie lay loosely around his neck, giving him an air of infuriating relaxation that was completely at odds with the icy hardness of his face. She was pleased to notice that there was a muscle flickering in the hollowed plane of his cheek.

'You don't strike me as a girl who likes to try too hard to get what she wants,' he said scathingly.

The injustice of the statement was so magnificent she almost laughed. Pressing her lips together, she had to look down for a second while she fought to keep a hold on her composure. 'Don't I?' Her voice was polite, deceptively soft as she met his gaze. 'Well, may I suggest that your assumption says more about you than it does about me, Alejandro?'

He flinched slightly, almost imperceptibly, as she said his name, and for a moment some unfathomable emotion flared in his eyes. But it was gone before she could read it or understand its meaning, and she was left staring into hard, golden emptiness. It was mesmerizing, like meeting the eyes of a panther at close range. A scarred, hungry predator.

'What does it say about me?'

He spoke quietly, but there was something sinister about his calmness. Above the immaculate, hand-made dress shirt his black eye and swollen mouth gave his raw masculinity a dangerous edge. Tamsin felt fear prickle on the back of her neck, and was aware that she was shaking.

Which was ridiculous. She wasn't *afraid* of Alejandro D'Arienzo. She was *angry* with him. Clenching her jaw, she managed a saccharine smile. 'Let me see,' she said with sugared venom. 'It says that you're an arrogant, misogynist bastard who thinks that women are for one purpose and one purpose only.'

His mouth, his bruised, sexy mouth, curled slightly in the barest, most insolent expression of disdain. 'And don't you rather perpetuate that stereotype?'

Tamsin felt the ground shift beneath her feet. The panelled walls seemed to be closing in on her, leaving her no chance of escape, no alternative but to confront the image he was holding before her of herself the girl who dressed like a slut and had thrown herself at him without even bothering to tell him her name.

'That was six years ago,' she protested hoarsely. 'One night, six years ago!'

'And how many times has it happened since then?' he said, draining his glass and picking up another cue.

Surreptitiously holding the edge of the green-baize table, Tamsin took a quick, shaky breath and made herself hold her head high as she gave a nonchalant shrug. The entire contents of the Cartier shop window wouldn't induce her to let him see how much his rejection had hurt her, how far-reaching its consequences had been. She managed a gratifyingly breezy laugh.

'I don't know, it's hardly a big deal. Don't try to tell me you've lived a life of monastic purity and celibacy for the last six years?'

He didn't look at her. 'I'm not going to.'

'Well, don't you think it's a bit much to expect that I have? What did you think, Alejandro, that I would have hung up my high heels and filled my wardrobe with sackcloth and ashes just because you weren't interested?' She laughed, to show the utter preposterousness of the idea. 'God, no. I moved on.'

'So I saw. A number of times, evidently,' he drawled quietly, bending down and lining up a shot. 'The England squad seems to be your personal escort-agency.'

Idly he jabbed the cue against the white ball, sending it hurtling across the table. Tamsin felt like it was her heart. 'Wrong, Alejandro,' she said stiffly. 'The England squad are my *clients*.'

His eyebrows shot up; he gave a twisted smile. 'Indeed? My mistake. I got it the wrong way round.'

'Don't be stupid,' she snapped. 'They're my clients because I'm the designer who handled the commission for the England kit. The new strip, the suits and the off-pitch clothing.'

Just for the briefest second she saw a look of surprise pass across his deadpan face, but it was quickly replaced by cynicism again.

'Did you, indeed?' he drawled, somehow managing to make those three small, innocuous words convey his utter disbelief. But before Tamsin had a chance to think up a suitably impressive response the door burst open and Ben Saunders appeared, swaying slightly. His unfocused gaze flitted from Alejandro to Tamsin.

'Oops. Sorry... Interrupting.' Grinning, obviously misreading the tension that crackled in the quiet room, he began to back out again with exaggerated care, but Tamsin leapt forward, grabbing his arm.

'Ben, wait!' she said grimly. 'Tell *him*—' she jerked her head sharply in Alejandro's direction '—about the new strip. Tell him who designed it.'

Frowning, Ben looked drunkenly at her as if she'd just asked him to work out the square root of nine hundred and forty two in binary.

'Uh...you?' he said uncertainly.

Great, thought Tamsin hysterically. *Brilliant. Hugely convincing*.

'Yes. Of course it was me,' she said with desperate patience.

Ben nodded and grinned inanely, obviously relieved to have got the right answer. 'And the shoots,' he slurred, turning around clumsily to show off his suit, and almost overbalancing. 'You did the shoots too, didn't you? Lovely shoot.' He beamed across at Alejandro. 'Very clever, Tamsin. Very good at measuring the inside leg...'

Alejandro glanced at her, his face a study of sadistic amusement. 'I'm sure,' he said icily. 'That takes a lot of skill.'

Tamsin clenched her teeth. 'Thanks, Ben,' she said, turning him around and steering him towards the door. 'Now, maybe you'd better go and find some water, or some coffee or something.' When the door had closed behind him she turned back to

Alejandro with a haughty glance. 'There. Now do you believe that I'm not just some airhead heiress with time on her hands?'

'It proves nothing.' Malice glinted in the golden depths of Alejandro's eyes as he picked up his glass again. 'I'm sure it makes great PR sense for you to be used as a front for the new strip, but surely you don't expect me to believe that you actually designed it? Sportswear design is an incredibly competitive business, you know.'

'Yes.' Tamsin spoke through gritted teeth. 'Astonishingly enough, I do know, because I got the job.'

Nodding thoughtfully, Alejandro took an unhurried mouthful of his drink. 'And what qualified you for that, Lady Calthorpe—your father's position in the RFU? Or your own extensive research into rugby players' bodies?'

'No,' she said as soon as she could trust herself to open her mouth without screaming. 'My first class honours degree in textiles and my final year project on techno-fabrics.' Looking up at him, she gave an icy smile. 'I had to compete for this commission and I got it entirely on *merit*.'

His dark brows arched in cynical disbelief. 'Really?' he drawled. 'You must be good.'

'I am.'

It was no use. If she stayed a moment longer, she wouldn't be able to keep the rip tide of vitriol that was swelling and surging inside her from smashing through her flimsy defences. She put down the cue and threw him what she hoped was the kind of distant, distracted smile that would convey total indifference as she turned to reach for the doorknob. 'You don't have to take my word for it, though. If you look at my work, it should speak for itself.'

'I have, and it does. For the rugby shirts, at least.' He laughed softly and she froze, her hand halfway to the door as a bolt of horrified remembrance shot through her. 'I have one, remember?'

Her fingers curled into a fist and she let it fall to her side, the nails digging painfully into her palm. She could have sunk down onto the thick, wine-red carpet and wept. Instead she steeled herself to turn back and face him.

'Of course,' she said, unable to keep the edge of bitterness from her voice. 'How could I forget?'

He came slowly towards her, his head slightly to one side, an expression of quiet triumph on his face. 'I really don't know, since you seemed pretty keen to get it back earlier,' he said quietly. 'Obviously it can't be that important, after all. To you, anyway.'

Tamsin swallowed. He had come to a halt right in front of her, and it was hard to marshal the thoughts swirling in her head when it suddenly seemed to be filled with *him*. She closed her eyes, trying to squeeze him out, but the darkness only made her more aware of his closeness, the warm, dry scent of his skin. She opened them again, looking deliberately away from him, beyond him, anywhere but at him.

'It *is* important, I'm afraid. I need it back.'

'You *need* it?' he said softly. 'If you're the designer, you must have lots of them. Surely you can spare that one?'

'It's not that simple. I…'

The mirror above the fireplace reflected the broad sweep of his shoulders, the silk of his hair, dark against the collar of his white shirt. She stared at the image, mesmerised by its powerful beauty as the words dried up in her mouth.

'No. I thought not,' he cut in, a harsh edge of bitterness under-cutting the softness of his tone, like a knife blade wrapped in velvet. 'It's not about the shirt, is it? It's about the principle—just as it always was. It's about your father not wanting the English rose on an Argentine chest, isn't it?'

Argentine chest. *Alejandro's chest.*

'No,' she whispered.

Gently, caressingly, he reached out and slid his warm hand along her jaw, cupping her face, stroking his thumb over her cheek. A violent shudder of reluctant desire rippled through her. She felt herself melt against him for a second before his fingers closed around her chin, forcing her head back so she was looking straight into his hypnotic eyes.

'I hope you're a better designer than you are a liar.'

'I'm not lying,' she hissed, jerking her head free. Her hand automatically went to the place where his had just been, rubbing the skin as if he had burned her. 'This has nothing to do with my father. There was a—a problem with the production of the shirts. I only found out yesterday when I suddenly thought to test one, and found out the red dye on the roses wasn't colourfast. I had to contact the manufacturers and get them to open up the factory and start from scratch on a new batch of shirts, but there was only time to make one for each player. *That's* why I need yours back, otherwise on the photoshoot at Twickenham tomorrow Ben Saunders will be half-naked, as well as hungover,' she finished savagely, feeling her blood pressure soar as he gave a short, cruel laugh. 'What's so funny?'

'I thought you were supposed to be good: "I had to compete for this commission and I got it entirely on merit",' he mocked. 'So who exactly were you competing against, Tamsin? Primary school children?'

'Oh, I can compete with the best, make no mistake about that,' she said with quiet ferocity, which melted seamlessly into biting sarcasm as she added, 'Now, it's been just *fabulous* to see you again, Alejandro, but I really ought to be getting back to the party. So if you could just give me back the shirt?'

She was walking towards the door as she spoke, but suddenly he was in front of her, blocking her path. Looking up, Tamsin saw with a shudder that all trace of amusement had vanished from his face. His eyes were as cold and hard as Spanish gold.

'Sorry. The spoiled-diva routine won't work with me.'

Misery and resentment flared up inside her, and for a moment she could do nothing but look at him. 'What do you want me to do? Beg?'

Kicking the door shut, he took a step towards her and she shrank backwards, pressing herself against the billiard table. 'It's quite a nice idea,' he said thoughtfully. 'But I think not, on this occasion.' He leaned forward, as if he were about to touch her. She flinched away with a low hiss of animosity, but he was only reaching for something behind her.

'So, you reckon you can compete with the best, do you?' he said softly. 'Let's see if you were telling the truth about that, at least.'

He handed her the billiard cue he had picked up from the table. Hesitantly, Tamsin took it, looking up at him in mute uncertainty.

'I don't understand. What are you saying?'

'You want your shirt back? You have to win it.'

CHAPTER FOUR

FOR just the briefest second he saw panic flare in her eyes, and felt an answering surge of grim satisfaction.

'Don't be ridiculous,' she snapped, looking at the cue as if it was a loaded gun. 'Play now? With *you*?' She gave a harsh, scornful laugh. 'Forget it.'

Chips of ice crystallised in Alejandro's heart. He was offering her a chance to prove herself. She couldn't hope to win, of course; he was far too skilled a player for that. But he would have given her credit—and the shirt back—just for trying.

And giving Tamsin Calthorpe credit for anything went very much against the grain.

'Afraid of losing?' he said scathingly. 'I don't blame you. I don't suppose you're used to it, and, believe me, I won't make allowances for who you are—or who your father is.'

Brimstone sparked in the depths of her green eyes. 'It's not the thought of losing that bothers me,' she hissed. 'It's the prospect of spending the next hour in your company.'

'Oh, don't worry,' he said, his voice a languid drawl. 'It won't take that long for me to thrash you.'

He was only inches away from her. Close enough to hear her little shivering gasp, close enough to see the instant darkening of her eyes as his words hit her and the flashing anger was swallowed by spreading pools of desire at their centre.

'Thrash me?' She gave a hoarse laugh. 'I don't think so.'

His eyebrows rose. 'You're walking away?'

'Oh no,' she breathed. Reaching out, she curled her fingers around the cue he held and for a moment came so close to him that he could feel the warm whisper of her breath on his neck. 'I'm not going anywhere. Not until I have my shirt back.'

Languidly she turned and walked away from him to the other end of the table. Alejandro frowned, feeling his chest, and his trousers tighten as he watched the sinuous movement of her bare back. He hadn't expected this.

'So, what are we playing?' she said, whipping round to face him again. 'Bar-room pool?'

The low light from the billiard lamp fell onto her short platinum-blonde hair, making her look like a rebellious angel. She was looking at him steadily, insolently, her head lowered slightly and her slanting green eyes unblinking.

'If that's what you want.'

She shrugged. 'I'm easy. I just thought it might be what you're used to.'

For a fleeting second Alejandro felt almost lightheaded with hatred at her casual, calculated viciousness. To her, he was still the boy from nowhere, the imposter in the charmed circle of privileged English youth that made up the team, and her social circle.

'I can play anything, anywhere, *Lady* Calthorpe. Would you prefer English billiards perhaps?'

His voiced dripped with contempt and his eyes raked over her, cold and assessing. Holding the cue upright in front of her, Tamsin clung to it tightly, glad of its support. English billiards? How the hell did you play that?

'No. Bar-room pool is fine with me,' she said, trying to make it sound of little consequence to her, but secretly hoping that all those smoky afternoons spent playing pool in the student bar at college were about to pay off.

She was in danger of getting seriously out of her depth here.

With the lamplight casting hollows beneath his razor-sharp cheekbones and the bruising on his lip, he looked like some kind of avenging warrior, primed for battle. Her hands were damp as she watched him move easily around the table. *I can play anything, anywhere,* he'd said, and she knew with a sick, churning mixture of fear and excitement that he was right. He would be just as at home playing pool in the back-street bars of Buenos Aires as playing billiards in an upmarket gentlemen's club in Mayfair. He exuded an effortless confidence that transcended all boundaries and singled him out as a natural winner.

Which was unfortunate, considering her reputation kind of rested on getting this shirt back.

'You first.'

Placing her right hand firmly on the table, Tamsin hoped he couldn't see how much it was shaking.

'You're left-handed?'

'In some things.'

She took the shot, mis-hitting wildly so that the balls scattered crazily over the table.

'You're sure this is one of those things?' Behind her his was voice cold and mocking. 'Maybe you might be better with your right hand.'

She turned, colour seeping into her cheeks as a slow pulse of anger beat in her veins. 'Thanks for the tip, but can we assume that if I want your help I'll ask for it?'

'I thought I'd already made it clear that, even if you did, you wouldn't get it,' he said smoothly, moving around the table and potting balls with a swift, lethal efficiency that made Tamsin's heart plummet. 'Although maybe I could make it a little fairer.' He smiled lazily across the table, moving his cue to the other hand. 'Since you're playing left-handed, I will too. Number ten. To you.'

Tamsin opened her mouth to make some stinging retort, but found her throat was dry and no words came. Helplessly her gaze fixed itself on the strong, tanned hand Alejandro placed on the table, splaying his lean, long fingers.

The room was very quiet and very still. A clock ticked on the mantelpiece, below which the fire had sunk to an amber glow.

His narrow, focused stare was exactly level with her knicker line, and it was intense enough to feel like he could see right through the flimsy grey chiffon.

The thought sent a gush of arousal crashing through her.

The sudden sharp crack of the balls colliding made her jump, and she watched, mesmerized, as the yellow ball rolled gently across the green baize towards the pocket beside her thigh. A shiver rippled through her as she suddenly, unaccountably, found herself thinking not of the movement of the ball across the table, but of Alejandro's fingers over her skin...

Guiltily she wrenched her head up as the ball came to a halt. Alejandro was watching her, the expression on his dark, bruised face unreadable.

'There,' he said with exaggerated courtesy. 'Your turn.'

Tamsin blinked. He'd missed the shot. That was good news, but somehow the knowledge that he'd only missed because he'd taken it with his left hand took any sense of triumph she might have felt and turned it right on its head.

'I don't need favours, Alejandro, and I don't need special treatment,' she snapped, walking briskly towards him to take the shot. 'In fact, let's be honest, I don't need any of this. Wouldn't it be better for both of us if you just did the decent thing for once in your life and gave the shirt back to me now? Or are you on some kind of personal mission to make my life as unpleasant and difficult as possible?'

'You want to concede defeat?'

There was a sinister, watchful stillness about him, and his tone was carefully neutral, but she heard the challenge in his words.

She smiled slowly, sweetly. Adrenalin was pulsing through her like pure alcohol, dilating her blood vessels, making her heart beat faster. She felt high, but at the same time perfectly lucid and oddly calm as she turned her body towards his, mirroring his position, leaning with one hip propped against the edge of the table. 'You'd love that, wouldn't you?' she said softly. 'Which is exactly why it's the last thing I'd ever do.'

He didn't smile back. His swollen upper lip accentuated the beauty of his face while making him look twice as dangerous. Standing there, with the lamplight making the hair that fell over his face blue-black, he was every inch the Spanish *conquistador*.

'You're sure about that?' he said quietly, almost apologetically. 'You have to know that you don't have a snowball's chance in hell of winning this?'

He held her in his gaze. It was like drowning slowly in warm syrup…delicious…but no less terrifying for it. She blinked. Drowning was drowning, after all.

'Let's see, shall we?' she said in a low voice, and moved round so that she was facing the table again. She was acutely, painfully aware of him beside her, towering over her as she bent to take her shot, looking down on her bare back with that hard, golden gaze that seemed to warm her skin like evening sun.

She had to get a grip. Concentrate.

There was no hurry. She flexed her shoulders slightly, steadying herself. Above her she heard a low rasping sound as Alejandro dragged a hand across his stubble-roughened jaw. She clamped her own mouth shut against the whimper of excitement that rose up in her at the sound, and took the shot.

With a series of satisfying staccato clicks, the balls ricocheted around the table, the orange she'd lined up cannoning neatly into the top pocket. She threw him a quick glance from under her lashes as she moved around to the other side of the table.

'I hope you're keeping score.'

Alejandro gave a low, ironic laugh. 'Don't worry about that. And you still have a long way to go before the shirt is yours. Don't get complacent.'

The look she gave him was full of fire and loathing. Alejandro watched with interest as she bent forward over the table to take the next shot, his eyes automatically travelling to the shadowed hollow between her breasts. Being so relentlessly spoiled for a lifetime had obviously given her a completely unrealistic grasp of her own limitations, he mused, forcing himself to shift his gaze upwards to her face. In the glow of the lamp above, the green baize of the table intensified the colour of her eyes to a vivid emerald. He watched them flicker, dart, measuring the distance as a tiny frown of concentration appeared between them.

She hesitated, completely focused, the tip of her pink tongue appearing between her plump lips. She moved, and with one swift flick of her wrist the ball dropped into the pocket. As it fell, Alejandro realised he'd been holding his breath. His whole body felt tense.

Well, that was one word for it. And some parts felt more 'tense' than others.

Damn her. As she straightened up he saw the same look of self-satisfied triumph on her face as he'd seen earlier in the hallway with her father when she'd got her own way. She was playing him, he thought acidly. She was perfectly aware of how sexy she looked, leaning over that table with her dress falling forward, and her green eyes right on a level with his crotch. She was manipulating him as ruthlessly as she had that night at Harcourt Manor all those years ago, but with twice as much finesse.

'This isn't complacency, Mr D'Arienzo,' she said huskily. 'This is confidence.'

Lust gripped him, making him feel dizzy. Leaning against the wall, tipping his head back, he watched through narrowed eyes as she undulated around the table, taking shot after shot. In the quiet room, everything seemed distorted, exaggerated, so that he was almost painfully aware of the soft sigh of her breathing, the whisper of chiffon against her velvet skin.

She straightened up. 'How many times do I have to tell you I don't want special treatment?' she said coldly. 'I missed. It's your turn.'

Scowling, he levered himself upright and walked stiffly around the table. His mind had been so occupied with other things he'd almost forgotten about the game, and he was surprised to see how few balls remained now. She was more skilled than he'd thought. As he leaned over the table he was aware of her picking up the small cube of chalk and rubbing it across the tip of her cue. He looked up. She was holding the cue in both hands in front of her, like a pornographic prop, and as he watched she put it by her mouth and blew softly, getting rid of the excess chalk.

It was deliberate torment.

'I have to congratulate you. You're quite a player.'

He spoke with lethal calm, but the careless savagery of his shot gave some hint of the choking rage inside him. The few remaining balls ricocheted violently from cushion to cushion and then stilled.

'Thank you.'

Alejandro took a step backwards, out of the pool of light, and leaned against the wood-panelled wall. Tensing his jaw, he looked away as she stood with her back to him to take her turn. 'It wasn't a comment on your sporting ability.'

Inexorably he found his head moving round to look at her again. In the lamplight from above her bare skin gleamed, as smooth and flawless as thick cream. The bones of her spine showed through, making him want to run his fingers down them to where they disappeared beneath the grey satin band of her dress. She shifted her position slightly, pressing her hips against the table and adjusting her weight in the high heels.

'No?' Her voice was cool and detached as she parted her legs to gain better balance and stretched forward over the table. He'd thought her legs were bare, but now he could see that he'd been wrong. She was wearing stockings of the sheerest silk. Stockings with wide, lace tops which were visible as she bent forward.

Alejandro felt his breath stop and his muscles tighten, as if he'd just been tackled and brought down. Hard.

She turned back to him and her eyes were very dark. 'What was it, then, Alejandro?'

'I was referring more to your match technique,' he said with quiet brutality. 'Though the theory behind it is fatally flawed. If you think that after last time there's even the smallest chance that I'd be interested—'

'You *bastard*!'

He caught her by the wrist as she raised her hand to hit him and wrenched her arm back to her side. Her breathing was very rapid, and he could feel the rise and fall of her chest against his own. 'Oh no,' she breathed, her voice trembling slightly. 'I wouldn't think that after last time there's any chance of that, Alejandro. Your lack of *interest* then was sufficiently spectacular to leave me in no doubt about that. But don't worry,' she went on, her emerald eyes glittering with feverish defiance, 'I'm sure that to most people all that hugging and kissing on the pitch when you score a try just looks like the camaraderie of the game.'

His grip tightened on her wrist, and he saw her wince. 'Be careful, Tamsin.'

She laughed, a low, breathy, mocking laugh. 'Why? Because you don't want—'

She didn't get any further. In one decisive movement Alejandro had closed the small gap that separated them and brought his mouth down on hers, so that the rest of her stupid, childish taunting was lost in the wildfire of his brutal kiss.

It was like falling off a cliff and finding she could fly. The ground beneath her feet melted away. Gravity ceased to exist. There was nothing but darkness and fire, and the roar of blood in her head. His fingers dug into her shoulders, pulling her against the hardness of his body. Of his arousal.

His rigid, obvious arousal.

Oh, God…

She wasn't aware of dropping the billiard cue, but she must have done, because suddenly her hands were sliding across the rock-hard contours of his shoulders, moving up the column of his neck to tangle into his hair. The taste of him, the scent of him, filled her— dry and masculine, earthy and clean. His mouth ground down on hers, violent, desperate, brilliant, searing his brand on her forever.

The billiard table pressed hard into her bottom and instinctively, with a hitch of her hips, she raised herself up so that she was sitting up on it, parting her thighs and pulling him into her.

The bittersweet taste of blood was on her lips, metallic and warm, and his fingers bruised her skin. She didn't care.

If he stopped now she knew she would scream.

She wriggled back on the table, grabbing the open collar of his evening shirt, pulling him with her. Suddenly she was aware of the sound of their breathing, harsh and laboured. Her whole body vibrated with want, arching towards him, opening like some exotic, fleshy flower, oozing nectar. Reality was irrelevant. The past was meaningless and the future incomprehensible. All that mattered was now, and this—the glorious incarnation of every one of her guilty, luscious teenage fantasies.

She was in the arms of Alejandro D'Arienzo, and his mouth was crushing hers, his hands holding her, sliding downwards, his thumbs caressing the underside of her breasts.

Alejandro lifted his head and looked at her. His eyes were as dark as vintage cognac, glinting dully in the low light, and his mouth was full and crimson where the ferocity of their kiss had opened up the cut in his lip.

He moved his thumbs upwards, brushing them over the hardened tips of her swollen, tingling breasts. She stiffened, her head falling backwards. Instinctively, helplessly, she felt her legs wrap around his body, tightening and drawing him into her, wriggling against him as the straining peak of his arousal pushed against the damp silk of her pants.

Her mouth opened in silent bliss, her eyes were wide, dazed, and her breathing shallow as, frozen on the brink of some terrifying, tempting abyss, she stared up into his bruised face.

His bruised, cold, totally emotionless face.

Before she could move or speak he had let her go, stepping sharply away from the table where she was sprawled backwards, turning so she could no longer see his face.

'I think we've proved that your cheap shots were wide of the mark, sweetheart,' he said mockingly. 'It's not that I'm not interested in women, *per se*. It's just that spoiled little girls who use sex as a bargaining tool don't really do it for me. Sorry.'

Points of light danced in front of Tamsin's eyes and for a desperate, horror-struck moment she thought she might faint. Or be sick.

She closed her eyes, fighting the feeling, focusing all of her fading energy on holding onto that small scrap of tattered dignity which would enable her to hold up her head and look him in the eye as she told him exactly what she thought about men who treated women like laboratory rats to be experimented on.

But when she opened her eyes again he was gone.

CHAPTER FIVE

TAMSIN gave a low moan of despair as she looked at her reflection in the big, cruelly lit mirror.

The lighting in the ladies' loo at Twickenham might be designed for functionality rather than flattery, but there was no doubt that the face that looked back at her was a mess. Mortuary-pale, with matching white lips, the only hint of colour came from the bluish shadows beneath her bloodshot eyes. It wasn't a good look.

Right at that moment she would rather face a firing squad—than photographers and journalists from the sports desk of every major national and special-interest publication in the country, but she didn't have much choice. Her father, along with members of the England management, was waiting for her, and he would expect her presentation to be seamless.

With a shaking hand she dabbed some lipstick onto her pale, numb lips and pressed them together, remembering with a slice of sudden breathtaking pain how they'd swelled and burned beneath Alejandro's kiss last night as the blood from his torn mouth had crimsoned them.

No.

She couldn't go there now, not when she had to get out there and look like a poised professional instead of the creature from the crypt. It was absolutely not the time to revisit the ground she had worn bare throughout the long hours of the night as she had asked herself the same question over and over again.

Why had she been so stupid?

Letting him humiliate and reject her once was bad enough. Giving him the opportunity to do it a *second* time… Well, that was nothing short of insanity. And yet, at the time she had been powerless to stop it. It was as if, the moment he'd left her shivering in the freezing darkness of the orangery at Harcourt, she had shut down and had gone into a state of mental suspended-animation. She remembered reading somewhere that extreme shock could do that to people. For six years she had gone about her life, looking for all the world like a normal person, a perfectly healthy, successful young woman, so that even those closest to her—even Serena—had no idea that beneath the surface she was frozen. A stopped clock.

Until last night.

Putting the lid back on the lipstick, she threw it into her bag and pressed her palms to her cheeks as tears smarted in her eyes again. *Big girls don't cry*: that was what her father always said. By the time Tamsin had been born Serena, two years older, had already cornered the market on 'pretty and feminine'. Tamsin did 'tough' instead, and Henry had accepted her as the son he'd never had. Tears were for babies, he'd told her, and Tamsin had learned very early to hold them in.

Last night had been a minor blip—well, quite a major blip, actually—but she was back on track today. She stepped back, taking a deep breath and giving herself one last look in the mirror before heading back out there. As a designer, her clothes were about so much more than fashion, both mirroring her mood and influencing it. The way she dressed always made a statement, and today's severe black trouser-suit said very loudly 'don't mess with me'. The four-inch heels she wore with it added, 'or I'll smash your face in'.

The noise from the press room spilled out along the corridor as she left the sanctuary of the ladies', a loud babble of conversation, as rowdy and excited as the bar on match day. Tamsin shuddered. Right now it sounded good-natured enough, but she had a horrible feeling that in a few minutes it could turn into the sound of a pack of journalists baying for her blood.

'Ah, there you are, Tamsin. We were waiting.' Henry Calthorpe looked at his watch as he came towards her. 'Is everything all right?'

Tamsin summoned a smile. It felt like strapping on armour plating. 'Everything's fine, Daddy,' she said ruefully. 'Why wouldn't it be?'

'No reason.' Henry was already moving away. 'You look pale, that's all. But if you're ready let's get started.'

The noise level in the press room rocketed as they filed in. The cameras started whirring and journalists got to their feet, keen to get their questions answered.

Boards showing life-size images of the players lined up at the start of yesterday's game had been placed behind the long table at the front of the room. Taking a seat right in front of Matt Fitzpatrick's hulking figure in the picture, Tamsin found herself sitting between her father and Alan Moss, the team physio. He was there to comment on the effect the techno-fabric of the new strip was expected to have on the players' physical performance, but he'd also come in very handy if she passed out, Tamsin thought shakily, picking up the pen that had been left on the table in front of her and starting to sketch.

Henry introduced them all, saying a few brief words about each person's role in the new team. When he reached Tamsin, the reporters seemed to strain forwards, like greyhounds in the stalls the moment before the start of the race.

'As you may be aware, Tamsin Calthorpe won the commission to design the new strip, as well as the off-field formal attire of the team.'

'Surprise, surprise!' shouted someone from the back. 'I wonder how that happened?'

Outrage fizzed through Tamsin's bloodstream. Instantly her spine was ramrod straight, her fingers tightening convulsively around the pen in her hand as her body's primitive 'fight or flight' instinct homed in on the former option. Forcing a grim smile, she looked into the glittering dazzle of flashbulbs in front of her.

'It happened thanks to my degree in textiles and my experience designing for my own label, Coronet.' She didn't quite manage to keep the edge of steel from her voice. 'I believe there were three other designers competing for the commission, and the selection process was entirely based on ideas submitted for the brief.'

'But why did you put yourself forward?' someone at the front persisted. 'You're best known for designing evening dresses worn by celebrities on the red carpet. It's quite a leap from that to top-level sports kit, wouldn't you say?'

She'd been expecting this question, and yet the hostility of the tone in which it was asked seriously got to her. She wondered if the microphone just in front of her was picking up the ominous thud of her heart.

'Absolutely,' she said through clenched teeth. 'And that was exactly why I wanted the commission. I'd built up my own label from nothing, and I was ready for the next challenge.'

'Was it the challenge you wanted, or the money? Rumour has it that the recent spate of high-street copies has hit Coronet hard.'

Tamsin felt like she'd been punched in the stomach. The bright lights of the cameras made it hard to see anything beyond the front row, but that was probably just as well. Lying was easier if you didn't have to make eye contact.

'Coronet's designs are as in demand as ever,' she said coldly. 'My business partner, Sally Fielding, is already handling requests for next year's Oscars and BAFTAs.'

All that was true. Sally had been approached by several stylists in Hollywood and London, but, since all of them expected dresses to be donated for nothing more than the kudos of seeing them on the red carpet, it didn't help Coronet's cash flow. But there was no time to dwell on that now. If she let her focus lapse for a second this lot would tear her limb from limb.

'Would you agree that your background as a womenswear

designer had an obvious influence on this commission?' another voice asked.

Thank goodness; a straightforward question.

Tamsin was just about to answer when the speaker continued, assuming an outrageously camp tone. 'The oversized rose-motif and the dewdrops on the rugby shirts are simply to die for, aren't they?'

A ripple of laughter went around the room. Tamsin's patience was stretched almost to its limit.

'Maybe it might be an issue for any guys who aren't quite confident about their masculinity,' she said sweetly. 'Fortunately, that doesn't include any of the team. The dewdrops, as you call them, are small rubberised dots that maximize grip for line-outs and scrums. But you're right—my background in couture has been influential. The starting point for any design is the fabric, and this was no different. Working in association with Alan here, and experts in the States, we sourced some of the most technologically advanced fabrics in the world.'

The room was quieter now. People were listening, scribbling things down as she spoke. A bolt of elation shot through her. 'We started with tightly fitting base-layer garments beneath the outer kit,' she continued, her voice gaining strength. This was safe ground. Whatever poisonous comments people could make about who she was or where she came from, no one could say she didn't know her subject. 'These are made from a fabric which actually improves the oxygenation of the blood by absorbing negative ions from the player's skin. It also prevents lactic acid build up, improving performance and stamina.'

'So why did England lose yesterday?' someone sneered from the back.

Because Alejandro D'Arienzo was playing for the opposition.

Tamsin's mouth was open, and for a terrible moment she thought she'd actually said that out loud. Casting a surreptitious, panicky glance around, she realised that the cameras were now pointing at the coach, who was talking about form, injury and training. Thank goodness. She picked up the mini bottle of water from the table in front of her and took a long mouthful, grateful for a moment of reprieve. On the pad in front of her she'd unconsciously been sketching the outline of an elongated female figure, and looking at it now she felt a wave of anguish. All the critics were right, she thought miserably, adding a drapey flourish of fabric falling from one shoulder of the figure. She didn't belong here. She should be back in the studio with all the team, working on next autumn's collection.

The pen faltered in her hand as dread prickled the back of her neck. If the business was still going then. The RFU commission had helped appease the bank a bit, but…

She gave a small start, dimly aware of Alan's gentle nudge. 'Tamsin? This one's for you.'

She blinked and looked ahead into the gloom beyond the dazzle of the camera lights. 'Sorry? Could you repeat the question, please?'

'Of course. I wondered—' the voice was leisurely, unhurried. '—did you encounter any particular problems in the production of the strip?'

A hand seemed to close around her throat so that for a moment she could hardly breathe, much less answer. There was no mistaking that deep, mocking, husky voice with its hint of Spanish sensuality. 'No,' she said sharply, her eyes raking the darkness, trying to locate him.

'None at all?'

He stepped forward, people standing around the edges of the room beyond the rows of chairs moving aside to let him through. His eyes, bruised and shadowed, burned into hers with laser-like intensity that belied the lazy challenge in his voice, and Tamsin noticed with a thud of sheer horror that in his hand he held the shirt.

The missing number-ten shirt.

The treacherous, sadistic, ruthless, vindictive *bastard*. For a moment she was speechless with loathing. He was trying to force her to admit, in front of people who were already cynical enough about her ability, that she had messed up.

As if he hadn't humiliated her enough.

'No,' she repeated coolly, lifting her chin and meeting his gaze head-on. 'I was lucky that the manufacturing team was excellent, and the whole production process was very straightforward. When working with very specialised fabrics like these, technical problems with dye or finishes are almost to be expected, but in this instance I managed to anticipate all potential issues and as a result there were no problems at all.'

There. She stared defiantly at him, daring him to say anything to the contrary. After all, if he did, that would betray the fact that he had inside information, which would be an extremely unwise move to make in front of a room full of journalists.

Tamsin's heart was pounding. She watched him glance down at the shirt in his hand, and back up again. Back at her. His face was like stone.

'I see. You had an excellent team. Does that mean that your involvement in this commission was merely nominal?'

'No, it does not,' she said in a low, fierce voice. Beside her, Tamsin heard her father make a sharp sound of impatience and disgust, and was aware of him leaning over to whisper something to the RFU official on his other side. She knew that at the smallest signal from her he would summon security to remove Alejandro D'Arienzo from the room, but the knowledge gave her no satisfaction. She didn't want him to go anywhere before she'd made him see that she was more than just a dizzy, vacant heiress playing at having a grown-up job.

'In that case,' said Alejandro smoothly, 'may I assume that you're available for other commissions of a similar kind?'

'What do you mean?'

The rest of the room was watching—waiting with the same morbid fascination that make people slow down when they passed a road accident, Tamsin thought bitterly. She felt like a cat who had been lured into the lion's cage at the zoo and was about to be devoured in front of a crowd of avid onlookers.

'Miss Calthorpe—sorry, *Lady* Calthorpe.' Alejandro's voice was husky, seductive, eminently reasonable. Only she could sense the barbs beneath the silk. 'You've convinced us all that you won this contract fairly and have been single-handedly responsible for seeing it through every stage from design to completion. I'm sure I'm not alone in admiring the results of your work.' There was a murmur of grudging assent from the rows of reporters. Tamsin felt irritation prickle up her spine as she noticed the rapt expressions on their faces as they looked up at Alejandro. 'I'm one of the sponsors of Los Pumas—the Argentine rugby team,' he was saying, 'And I'd like to invite you to redesign their strip for their relaunch next season.'

A moment ago they'd been preparing to lynch her, but one word from their hero and they were rolling over like puppies. It was sickening.

'I—sorry?'

Tamsin's head snapped round to look in bewilderment at her father as her mouth opened in astonishment. She should have been paying closer attention. For a moment there she thought he'd just asked her to design the Pumas strip, but surely she'd misheard?

Henry Calthorpe cleared his throat importantly. His voice was utterly dismissive. 'I'm afraid that would be impossible. Tamsin's schedule is booked up for months in advance, although I'm sure if you put your request in writing…'

A low, derisive murmur went around the room as the reporters shifted in their seats and looked meaningfully at each other, sensing carnage. But Tamsin was oblivious to everything but Alejandro. His dark, handsome face wore the look of a pirate king who had just forced the damsel in distress to walk right to the end of the plank.

There was nowhere for her to go, and he knew it. It was a case of give in, or give up. If she refused him now, it would make everything she'd just said sound like a lie.

Tamsin didn't give in easily, but she knew when she was out-manoeuvred. She forced herself to look straight at him, but it was more than she was capable of to manage a smile as well.

'I'd be absolutely delighted, Mr D'Arienzo.'

So, Tamsin Calthorpe had talent, of that there was no doubt. Whether it extended into the field of design, or was simply confined to deception and dishonesty remained to be seen.

Alejandro pushed through the crowd of journalists, many of whom had now turned in his direction to pick up on the unexpectedly juicy twist the story had just taken. Ignoring them, he made straight for the door through which the RFU officials, with Tamsin amongst them, had just disappeared.

He saw her straight away, deep in conversation with her father at the far end of the room where croissants and coffee were set out on a table. If that severe black trouser-suit was supposed to make her look grown up and professional, she'd got it completely wrong, he thought sourly. She just seemed absurdly young; far too thin and somehow…

Ah. Of course.

Vulnerable.

Silly of him to be so slow on the uptake. That was exactly the effect she must have been going for.

As he crossed the room towards them, he watched her put a hand on her father's arm, as if restraining him. Deliberately he avoided looking at Henry Calthorpe, instead focusing on his daughter. She was very pale—he'd thought before that was just the harsh TV lighting—but he could see now that she looked as if she were about to pass out. Could it be that he'd finally managed to shake the oh-so-secure world of Lady Tamsin?

Leaving Henry's side, she came over to him. She was trembling, he noticed with a twisting sensation deep in his gut.

'I hope you're satisfied.'

'Extremely,' he said in an offhand tone. 'I've just secured the services of an extremely talented designer who's apparently booked up for the foreseeable future. Now all I need is a cup of coffee and my day would be made.'

Her fine eyebrows rose. He could almost see the sparks of hostility that seemed to electrify the air around her. 'Secured? I'm sorry—shouldn't that be *blackmailed*?'

Alejandro laughed. 'You've been watching too many films. Or did I miss the part when someone held a knife to your throat?'

'You know what I mean,' she hissed, looking swiftly around her, as if checking to see if anyone was listening, and taking a step towards him. 'You know that there's no way I could refuse out there, with the world's press just waiting for a chance to tear me to ribbons.'

With some effort Alejandro kept his face and his voice completely blank. Her clean, floral scent as she moved closer gave him a sudden flashback to last night, and how it had felt to kiss her. His lip, swollen and bruised this morning, throbbed at the memory.

'Refuse? Now why would you want to do that?'

'Because I cannot and will not work for someone I don't respect.'

He moved past her, and with complete insouciance began pouring coffee from the cafetière on the table into a china cup. 'Oh dear,' he drawled. 'Well, you'd better get over the artistic-diva tantrums, because by tomorrow morning every paper is going to be carrying the story of how England's up and coming celebrity designer is off to Argentina to work her creative magic on the Pumas.' He turned back to her, leaning against the table as he took a thoughtful sip of coffee. 'Unless of course you'd like me to call some contacts and tell them you've reconsidered—'

'*Argentina?*' Her eyes widened in horror, 'Who said anything about Argentina?'

For a split second she looked so scared that Alejandro almost felt sorry for her. Almost. But the memory of what she'd done to him six years ago burned like his split lip. It was her turn to be sorry now.

'Did you really think I would bring the whole team over here? That may be how people in Tamsin's world usually operate, but you're going to have to get used to a whole new way of doing things, sweetheart.'

Watching her eyes darken from emerald to the dark, opaque green of yew trees in winter, he waited for the storm to break. He had seen from the little firework display last night when she'd tried to hit him that Lady Tamsin had a formidable temper, and wondered what she would do now. Scream? Throw something? Or turn to Daddy for help?

She tilted her chin, her blistering hostility cleverly cloaked in ice-cold nonchalance. Alejandro was grudgingly impressed at her restraint.

'Why are you doing this to me?'

'To you?' he said very quietly. 'Oh no, Tamsin, I'm doing it *for* you. I'm giving you a chance to prove yourself. I'm giving you a chance to showcase your talents and seal your reputation. You should be grateful. I thought you liked a challenge.'

She laughed softly then, almost as if she was relieved. It sounded breathy and musical. 'I get it. You think that I've had my hand held and all the hard work done for me here, don't you? You think that I'm going to be absolutely clueless out there on my own, and you just can't wait to watch me fail.' She looked up at him, her soft, pink mouth curved into a smile. 'Well, Alejandro, I won't fail. I did it all myself, and I can do it again— better, more easily this time—so, if you're dragging me over to the other side of the world just so you can have the pleasure of watching me screw up, you're wasting your time.'

'Fighting talk. Very impressive,' he drawled sardonically. 'But I warn you, Tamsin, this isn't a game. This isn't like last night, where you can flirt and seduce your way through when the going gets tough. This is work.'

A rosy tide flooded her cheeks and the smile evaporated instantly. 'And you're the boss, right?' she said with quiet venom. 'Good. I'm so glad we got that straight, because if you so much as lay a finger on me I'll have you for sexual harassment faster than you can say "hotshot lawyer".'

Before Alejandro could respond, a member of the grounds team in an England tracksuit and baseball cap had appeared beside them, looking anxious. 'Miss Calthorpe?' he said nervously. 'The photographer's ready to start the photo-shoot down on the pitch. But, er, unfortunately we seem to be missing one shirt…'

For a moment she didn't move. And then, still keeping her gaze fixed to his, she said, 'Thank you. I'm bringing it right now.'

Alejandro smiled as much as his swollen lip would allow. 'A car will come for you tomorrow morning,' he said with exaggerated courtesy. 'Please be ready by eleven o'clock.'

'Tomorrow? But—' She stopped abruptly, visibly struggling to rein in the furious protest that had sprung to her lips. Finally, pressing her lips together, she gave a curt nod and turned on her heel to follow the grounds official.

Alejandro watched her go, her narrow back ramrod-straight, her blonde head held very high. She was hanging onto that fiery temper by a thread, he thought wryly. She seemed very confident that she could handle the professional aspect of the next couple of weeks—but how would she do on the personal? Would the spoiled little diva be able to cope?

He waited until she was almost at the door before calling, 'Oh—and Tamsin?'

She turned, her face set into a mask of politeness. 'Yes, Mr D'Arienzo? Or, now I'm working for you, should I call you "sir"?'

'Alejandro is fine. We'll be flying on my private jet tomorrow. It's only a small plane, so bring one bag only, please. I know what women are like for packing ridiculous amounts of unnecessary clothes.'

The look she shot him was ice-cool. 'You're saying clothes will be unnecessary? Careful, Mr D'Arienzo—this is business, remember?'

And then she was gone. Alejandro was left staring after her, his coffee cooling in his hand, his mind swirling with disturbing thoughts of Tamsin Calthorpe sprawled naked on the leather seats of his jet, and the unwelcome suspicion that she'd just scored some victory over him.

He'd take her advice. He would be careful.

He had an uneasy feeling that this was going to be a whole lot more trouble than he'd bargained for.

CHAPTER SIX

'*ONE* bag! How the hell am I supposed to get everything I need into one stupid bag?' Wedging the phone against her shoulder, Tamsin picked up a soft jacket, the colour of dark chocolate, and looked at it longingly. 'Should I take my army coat or the brown cashmere jacket?'

'Cashmere,' said Serena firmly. 'The other one makes you look like you're in the Hitler Youth. So, tell me, how's Daddy about all this?'

'Well, that's another annoying thing, actually. He's *furious*. Which is particularly unfair, considering he knows I had absolutely no choice.'

She squashed the jacket onto the top of her already bulging leather holdall. It was half-past ten, and the bedroom looked like the scene of a police raid, with drawers pulled open and spilling out silken wisps of underwear, cardigans and dresses in every colour.

'Darling, since when has Pa been rational where his best beloved daughter is concerned? He thought he'd dealt with this problem once and for all, so you can't blame him for being a bit fed up.'

'What?' said Tamsin vaguely, looking around the room. 'Do you think three sweaters will be enough?'

'Sweaters?' There was a long silence at the other end of the phone. Eventually Serena said in a strangled voice, 'Tamsin, just run by me what else you've packed.'

Tamsin picked up a thick leather belt with a heavy jewelled

buckle and threw it back into a drawer. 'Look, I know you're going to say that I should take lots of dressy stuff, and that Alejandro Playboy D'Arienzo probably holds A-list parties every night or whatever, but I don't care, because I'm not getting involved in *any* of that. I'm not interested in him. I'm there to work.'

'It's not that. Just tell me you haven't packed for winter? Darling, it's the height of summer over there just now. The temperature is in the thirties!'

In the middle of the chaos Tamsin stopped and went very still, her mouth suddenly dry. Her eyes darted to the big, old-fashioned schoolroom clock on the wall by the window, and then to the miserable London greyness outside. She gave a small whimper.

'Oh, God. Oh, *no*! I didn't think…"

'OK. Don't panic. Let's be rational about this. First you have to take everything out of the bag.'

'Everything out,' repeated Tamsin desperately, pulling out armfuls of cashmere and wool and trying not to cry. 'OK. Now wh—?'

She stopped suddenly as she heard the sound of a car engine in the mews below.

He wasn't due for another fifteen minutes yet, and surely he wouldn't be so inconsiderate as to—?

A door slammed. Footsteps echoed on the frosty pavement.

'Oh, Serena. He's here,' she whimpered into the phone as the doorbell rang. 'What am I going to do?'

'OK,' said Serena urgently. 'You're going to be cool and professional. You're going to bear in mind at all times that he is absolutely not to be trusted, and most importantly of all—' the doorbell rang again '—you are *not* going to sleep with him.' She sighed. 'But first, you're going to let him in.'

'Finally.' Alejandro walked past her into the narrow hallway and looked around with barely concealed impatience. 'I was just about to leave. I assumed you'd had second thoughts.'

'About such a—what was it?—generous opportunity to prove myself?' Tamsin said sweetly. 'Now why would I do that?'

'You tell me,' he replied with heavy irony. 'Are you ready?'

She was halfway up the narrow stairs. 'Nope. Come up.'

Gritting his teeth in irritation, Alejandro followed her, trying not to look at her rear in the skinny black jeans she wore.

'This better not take long. My driver's waiting.'

'Really?' she said lightly. 'Can you drive to Argentina? I thought we'd be going by plane.'

He found himself in a large living space with windows all along one wall and warm old pine floorboards. There was a kitchen area at one end with peacock-blue cupboards and an enormous French baker's rack groaning under the weight of china and pans. The other end was taken up with a huge sofa upholstered in shocking pink brocade and a white furry rug. The whole space was painted in a creamy off-white, and even on the greyest winter morning it was airy and bright.

It was also incredibly messy.

'Have you been burgled, or is it always like this?' he asked, looking around. On the table beside the telephone was a pile of unopened brown envelopes, many of them printed in red and marked 'urgent'.

Stepping over piles of clothes, magazines, discarded shoes and scraps of fabric, he made his way to the door through which Tamsin had just disappeared and felt a dart of heat as he realised it was her bedroom.

'No, and no,' she said haughtily, picking up an armful of bulky winter clothes and shoving them into the bottom drawer of an enormous old *armoire*. 'It's like this because some annoying person forced me to travel halfway across the world at a moment's notice, and then arrived early to pick me up.'

Alejandro glanced at his watch. 'Ten minutes. That's hardly *early*. I assumed you would have packed last night.'

'Oh, did you?' she snapped. 'Well, I think that's one of the many things I find annoying about you, Alejandro. You have no right to assume anything. How do you know that I didn't have other plans last night? Why should I turn my life upside down and cancel everything when you snap your fingers?'

Without letting a flicker of the emotion that suddenly licked up through him at the thought of what her 'other plans' for last night had been, Alejandro bent down and picked up a scrap of fuchsia-pink silk from the floor beside the bed and held it up. It was a suspender belt.

'It doesn't look as if you cancelled anything last night,' he said sardonically, feeling a twist of grim satisfaction as he watched her eyes widen in outrage. For a moment she stared mutely at him as he turned the delicate band of silk and lace around in his hands before tossing it casually onto the bed.

'If you must know I spent last night in my design studio, alone, getting together all the stuff I need to bring with me for work. That's why I haven't had time to tidy up, or pack, because *that's why* I thought you'd hired me—to design your rugby strip for you. If you'd wanted someone with the domestic skills of Snow White, you should have gone to Disneyland.'

She had a point. Maybe he should have, because from what he'd found out last night it seemed likely that Snow White would be about as capable of designing sportswear as Lady Tamsin Calthorpe, and would probably be a lot less scared of hard work.

Leaning against the doorframe, Alejandro shoved his hands into his pockets and watched her thoughtfully. He knew from the press conference yesterday when she had so convincingly denied that there had been any problems with the production of the shirts that she was a virtuoso liar. In fact, identifying when she was telling the truth and when she was making it up was going to be very entertaining. The flight to Buenos Aires was fifteen hours. A challenge like that would pass the time nicely.

He sighed impatiently, letting his gaze wander around the room. The bed was an old Edwardian brass one, piled high with lace pillows and silk cushions, both its head- and footboards draped with sequined scarves, bead necklaces and bras. The intimate femininity of the place made him uncomfortable. It reminded him of things that he'd resolved to forget. A bottle of perfume on the antique dressing-table instantly brought back the warm, fresh scent of her body; a lidless lipstick beside it conjured an image in his mind of her lips, plump and pink in the moments before he'd kissed her, engorged with desire and scarlet with his own blood as he'd pulled away.

Levering himself away from the doorway in one sharp, aggressive movement, he crossed impatiently to the window. 'I suppose it's pointless telling you to hurry up.'

Tamsin gritted her teeth and very deliberately carried on folding the long linen shirt on the bed. 'If you helped it would be quicker,' she said with exaggerated patience. 'Or is helping anyone an entirely alien concept?'

Alejandro turned round. 'It depends,' he said slowly in a voice that dripped acid, 'whether the person you help is then going to claim they did it all themselves.'

The barb found its mark with cruel accuracy. Tamsin bit back a small gasp of pain and grabbed another plain-white linen shirt from the wardrobe, followed by a faded pair of cut-off jeans and an Indian-print tunic top. 'Forget it,' she muttered through clenched teeth. 'Just don't bother.'

'Don't forget this.' Alejandro picked up the suspender belt from where he'd thrown it on the bed and held it out to her. His eyes glittered with malicious amusement. Tamsin snatched it and shoved it viciously back in the drawer.

'I don't think I'll be needing that,' she said icily, gathering up a pale-blue satin bra and another one in pink candy-striped silk and throwing them in on top of the suspender belt. 'Or these. It's work, remember, Alejandro. I thought we made that perfectly clear.'

Ostentatiously she pulled out three pairs of plain-white cotton knickers, and a white cotton bra and, casting a defiant glance at Alejandro, threw them into the bag. Then she zipped it up.

'There. I'm done.'

'That's all you're taking?'

She saw him glance incredulously down at the bag, and shrugged nonchalantly to cover up her own sense of unease. Half an hour earlier it had been bursting at the seams, now it was half empty. But having Mr Disapproving there had really cramped her style. There was no way she was going to let him watch her pack anything that could remotely be considered frivolous or alluring.

'I think it's enough, since I don't intend to stay long, and I certainly don't intend to—'

He laughed. 'Enjoy yourself?'

'Absolutely.'

'Well, if you're sure you don't want to change your mind—add anything?'

'No. Let's just go.'

CHAPTER SEVEN

'SOME wine, Lady Calthorpe?'

Tamsin gave a stiff nod of assent. Squashing down a leap of annoyance at the use of her title, she watched Alberto, the uniformed steward, pour pale-gold wine into two long-stemmed glasses.

They'd been airborne for just over an hour, but in spite of the exceptional luxury of Alejandro's private jet she felt nervous and jittery. She'd spent all of the time so far gazing vacantly at a magazine, but couldn't remember a single detail of anything in it. She did, however, seem to have become oddly familiar with the cover of the share report which Alejandro was reading opposite her.

Alberto gave a courteous murmur and melted away, and Tamsin picked up her glass.

'Could you please inform your staff that there's absolutely no need to bother with the whole "Lady Calthorpe" thing?' she said brusquely. 'I never use the title myself, and I prefer it if other people just address me by my name.'

Alejandro looked up from the share report. 'Of course. If that's what you prefer, I'll pass it on.'

His face didn't betray a flicker of emotion, so why did Tamsin get the distinct impression that he was laughing at her? The irritation that had been simmering inside her for the last hour now came bubbling up, like milk coming to the boil.

'Do you have a problem with that?'

He leaned back in his seat, apparently totally relaxed, but his hooded gaze stayed fixed to her face with a sharpness that belied his laid-back body language. 'Not at all,' he said smoothly, throwing the report onto the seat beside him and unfolding a snowy-white linen napkin. 'I just find it slightly…ironic that you're suddenly so keen to play down your aristocratic connections.'

'Ironic?' she snapped. 'In what way *ironic*?'

Alejandro took an unhurried mouthful of wine. 'Well, you clearly have no problem with using them when it suits you, to get what you want.'

Alberto appeared again, carrying two white plates as big as satellite dishes, each bearing a delicate arrangement of pale-pink lobster and emerald-green salad leaves in its centre. He set these down on the table with elaborate care, giving Tamsin the chance to beat back the fury that instantly flamed inside her. She waited until Alberto had retreated again before answering.

'Let's get this straight from the outset, shall we? I love my family. I'm proud of who I am and where I come from, but I have *never* used it in any way to open doors for me in my professional life.'

Toying lazily with a rocket leaf, Alejandro reflected that that wasn't what the guy he'd had dinner with last night had said. A board member of the RFU, he had confided over an extremely good port that there had been no other contenders for the England-strip commission, that the design brief from the chairman's daughter had been the only one under consideration.

'You don't believe me, do you?'

He smiled. 'Not really. I'm prepared to believe that you might *think* that because you have a flat and a job that your life is just like everyone else's. But your family background—'

She cut him off with an incredulous gasp. 'You hypocrite! We're having this conversation on board your *private jet*, for God's sake! What do you know about living like everyone else?'

He felt himself tense, giving a small indrawn hiss of warning.

'The difference is,' he said with quiet venom, 'I've worked for this. For everything I have. I came from nothing, remember.'

He expected her to back down then, to understand that she—the pampered heiress who had never known what it was like to be without anything, particularly not an identity—was on very, very dangerous ground here. But she didn't. Instead she laid down her fork and looked at him through narrowed eyes.

'OK,' she said softly, pausing to suck mayonnaise off her thumb. 'You had it tough. So that made you need to prove yourself, didn't it?'

Her words were like a punch in the solar plexus. A very hard, accurate and unexpected punch.

'Which I'd say,' she went on in the same quiet, even tone, 'means that you're just as much shaped by your family background as I am.'

'Wrong. I have no "family background".'

His voice was like gravel, and the warning in it was blatant. She ignored it. A small frown creased her forehead beneath her sleek platinum hair, but other than that her expression was completely calm as she said, 'Of course you do. Everyone does.'

He gave an icy smile. 'Maybe in your world, but my *family background* was wiped out when I was five years old, when I came to England.'

Her frown deepened. 'Why did you come?'

The pressurised, climate-controlled air seemed suddenly to be charged with tension. Tapping one finger against the polished table top, Alejandro looked out at the blue infinity beyond the window of the plane. He wanted to tell her to back off, that she had strayed into territory that he kept locked, barred and guarded with razor wire, but somehow to do so felt like a denial of who he was and where he'd come from; a betrayal of his father.

And hadn't his mother betrayed Ignacio D'Arienzo enough for both of them?

He kept his tone neutral and his explanation brief. 'Argentina was a troubled country at the time that I was born. There was a military dictatorship. My father and uncles were taken for their involvement with a trade union, and my mother was afraid that we might be next. She was half English, on her father's side, and she booked us on a flight to London the next day. We took nothing with us.'

'What happened to your father?'

The pure, clear sunlight filtering in through the moisture-beaded window of the plane lit up Tamsin's face, turning her skin to translucent gold. She leaned forward, resting her elbows on the table and propping her chin upon them. Her eyes were the cool, shady green of an English woodland in summertime, and they seemed to draw him into their quiet depths.

'Who knows? He's one of thousands of *los desaparecidos*: the disappeared. Neither living nor dead.'

'That's an awful thing to have had to live with,' Tamsin said softly. 'Not knowing…'

He shrugged. 'It allowed me to believe that he was alive.' His smile was brutal. 'Unfortunately my mother didn't share that view. She remarried quite quickly—the man she worked for as a housekeeper in Oxfordshire.'

'Oh,' Tamsin said, and it was more of a whispered sigh than a word. She hesitated, biting her lip. 'But it can't have been easy for her.'

Alejandro rubbed a hand across his forehead. Of course, he should have realised that Tamsin Calthorpe would see it from his mother's side. They were two of a kind. Loyalty and faithfulness weren't on the program. It was all about expedience.

'Oh, I think it was,' he said with brittle, flinty nonchalance. 'I think it was very easy, in the end, to completely reinvent herself and behave as though the past had never happened. The only thing that was difficult was living with the reminder of where she'd come from. Which was where my long incarceration in the British public-school system began.'

While he was speaking she'd been playing absently with the stem of her wine glass, but suddenly she wasn't doing that any more, and her hand was covering his. Her touch seemed to burn him, to sear flesh that already felt exposed and flayed raw.

'I'm sorry,' she said in a quiet voice.

He'd waited six years for that, and the irony of the circumstances in which he was finally hearing it took his breath away. What was she sorry about—his mother's betrayal, or her own?

He moved his hand from beneath hers.

'I doubt it,' he said getting up and giving her a twisted smile. 'Yet.'

Well, actually, he was *wrong*. She was sorry. Very sorry.

Sorry she'd agreed to come with him, sorry she'd ever set eyes on him, sorry she'd made the mistake of responding to him like he was a decent, well-adjusted human being. It wouldn't happen again any time soon.

She was only trying to break down the awkwardness that seemed to exist perpetually between them. She was trying to be *nice*. She couldn't help it if he was bitter, emotionally arrested and had major trust issues.

Tamsin sighed and looked out of the window into nothingness. Major and perfectly understandable trust issues, she thought miserably. His revelations had touched her deeply, and she'd seen his pain behind the hard, cynical façade. She understood why he had so fiercely maintained his Argentine identity during his time in England, even though it had infuriated the management of the England team and had ultimately cost him his place on it. But it was all he had left of his father, and of his old life. He had been trying to stop himself disappearing too.

Beyond the window the light was fading, and the sky was the same leaden grey as the Atlantic Ocean far beneath them. With infinite weariness, Tamsin looked down at the magazine on her knee and read the same paragraph for the hundredth time. 'Next season's key trend will be camouflage', it said.

How appropriate, she thought, stifling a yawn with her hand.

'You're tired.'

She jumped as Alejandro's voice broke the thick silence that had lain between them for ages now. 'Get some sleep,' he said coolly. 'You know where the bedroom is.'

He had shown her when they had first boarded the jet, and she'd been utterly taken aback by such insane luxury. She'd like nothing more than to curl up now on the large bed—which was ridiculously out of proportion with the scaled-down proportions of the plane—and go to sleep, but Alejandro's faintly scornful tone made it impossible to admit that.

Straightening her spine, she blinked rapidly. 'I'm fine. It's your bed, you have it.'

'I have reading to catch up on. Business.'

His cold superiority made invisible hackles rise on the back of her neck. 'Yep. Me too,' she said briskly, picking up her laptop and flipping it open. 'Lots to be getting on with.' The sideways glance she shot him was filled with loathing, but her voice was deliberately sweet. 'After all, the sooner I make a start on this, the sooner I can go home again, and I think we'd agree that would be best all round.'

At least there was one thing they could agree on, Alejandro thought sourly, leaning forward to lower the blind on the window and block out the reflection of her face in the glass. As the darkness had deepened outside her reflection had gradually come to life, like a Polaroid photograph developing, and he had found his eyes were constantly drawn to it, noticing the way she chewed her bottom lip when she was reading, and how her fingers stroked the hair behind her ears.

All of which was completely irrelevant to the company he was currently thinking of buying, he thought scathingly, returning his attention to the share report.

Business was a game like any other, Alejandro had discovered. You had to observe the tactics of your opponents, recognise their strengths and exploit their weaknesses. You had to know when to hold back, and when to surge forward and press your advantage home. And you had to be able to do it without emotion.

He was good at all that.

Unconsciously now he found himself turning towards Tamsin, and felt an instant dropping sensation in his chest. She was sitting perfectly straight, her legs tucked up to one side of her on the wide leather seat, the laptop balanced on her thigh. The screen was blank, and her head was bent forward slightly so her long fringe fell down over her face.

She was asleep.

In one fluid movement Alejandro got out of his seat and crossed the narrow space between them, removing the computer from her knee and putting it on the table in front of her. Then, slipping one arm behind her neck, he slid the other beneath her knees and scooped her up, holding her against his chest.

Her head fell back, rolling against his arm and giving him a perfect view of her small face with its wide cheekbones and full, generous mouth. His heart gave a painful kick as he looked down at her. For six years he had painted her in his mind as a sort of cross between Lolita and Lady Macbeth, but it was impossible to reconcile that image with the soft, fragile girl in his arms. As he watched, her lips parted slightly and she gave a small, breathy sigh of contentment, and then tucked her head into his body.

With a low curse he turned abruptly and carried her to the back of the plane, kicking the door to the bedroom open and depositing her quickly on the bed. A cashmere blanket lay folded neatly at its foot, and he shook it out and laid it over her, briskly, his hands not making any contact with her body at all.

And then he left, as swiftly and as brutally as he had come, slamming the door shut behind him.

Tamsin's eyes snapped open the moment he was out of the small room.

A few seconds ago she'd been so tired she'd felt as if her eyelids had lead weights attached to them, but now she was wide, wide awake. Her heart was thumping against her ribs like a caged animal, and every cell of her body seemed to vibrate and thrum with painfully heightened awareness. It was as if someone had just injected her with concentrated caffeine.

Being in his arms for those few moments had done that to her.

She pushed back the blanket he had laid over her so perfunctorily and sat up, running her tongue over her dry lips and looking around her in something like desperation. When she'd felt his arms around her, felt the hardness of his broad chest against her, she'd thought for a dizzy, disorientated moment that she was dreaming and had given herself up to the bliss of being close to him...

Oh, no. She'd *sighed*, hadn't she? She'd actually sort of *moaned* with pleasure.

Springing up from the bed, she paced restlessly around it. She'd known it was going to be difficult, being thrown into such close contact with him, but she hadn't even come close to realising how hard. They were only halfway there, for crying out loud, and already she'd managed to make an almighty fool of herself—not once but twice.

Panic rose within her as she thought of the hours that stretched ahead, but there was no escape, and nothing to be done except try to keep her mind off Alejandro D'Arienzo altogether. Work was the answer, but her laptop was in the cabin, and there was no way she was going back out there to get it—although if she could just find some paper and a pen she could make a start on some sketches now. Her gaze fell on a little drawer set into the sleek cabinetry beside the bed, and she ran her fingers along it, trying to locate the concealed catch.

It sprang open, immediately revealing a blank notepad. Tamsin gave a little hiss of triumph as she took it out, looking underneath to see if she could see a pen.

There was one. Right there in the bottom of the drawer, half-buried beneath a lot of small, silver packets.

With a trembling hand she reached out and scooped them up, staring at them as a sick feeling spread through the pit of her stomach and an assortment of unwelcome images filled her head: Alejandro, his skin dark against the white sheets, his hair falling over his face as he lifted his mouth from the pouting, scarlet lips of a sultry beauty and reached over to the drawer for condoms.

The door handle turned with a muffled click. Tamsin gave a gasp of horror and slammed the drawer shut, stuffing the condoms into the back pocket of her jeans and spinning around as the door opened and Alejandro appeared.

'I thought I heard something. So, you're awake.'

'Of course,' she said as casually as possible, holding up the pad. 'As I said before, I've got work to do. I haven't got time to sleep.' She ran her shaking hands through her hair in the manner of someone who was perfectly relaxed and didn't have her pockets stuffed with condoms.

Alejandro advanced into the room. Apart from the fractional lift of his eyebrows his face was as expressionless as ever, but his eyes glittered with sardonic amusement. 'I see,' he said quietly. 'You were doing a pretty good impression of it before.'

'That wasn't sleep. That was a power nap.' Even to Tamsin's own ears her voice sounded ridiculously shaky, but she couldn't help it. It was the effect of being in this small space with him. This small, intimate space, with the huge bed stretching between them like a taunt, and the images conjured up by her own pitifully overactive brain refusing to go quietly. She turned away, hoping that it would help her keep her composure. 'I won't need proper sleep for ages now,' she said airily.

'Oh, you won't? That's good news.'

His voice was soft, hypnotising. Unwillingly, she felt herself turning back to face him. Unsmiling, he was looking at her steadily as he took hold of the bottom of his dark cashmere jumper and pulled it over his head. Tamsin's heart-rate doubled instantly and her mouth went dry.

'Why?' It came out as a hoarse croak. The pressurised air seemed to be filled with the sound of her throbbing heart.

His mocking smile was like icy water in her face.

'Because I assume that means you won't mind me having the bed.' He held open the door for her. 'Don't work too hard.'

* * *

The sky was pale pink by the time Tamsin set aside her laptop and rubbed her hands wearily across her face. Her eyes felt gritty and her head and neck ached with exhaustion, but she had a good basis for four different designs to show Alejandro and the board of Los Pumas. Letting her head fall back against the seat, she closed her stinging eyes and allowed herself a moment of triumph as she took a couple of deep breaths in, savouring the smell of fresh coffee that was coming from Alberto's galley kitchen, and the faint, skin-tingling scent of lime that was coming from…

Her eyes flew open. Alejandro was standing over her, smiling wryly. His hair was slicked back and damp from the shower, and in the golden morning sunlight he looked like something from an advert for men's expensive grooming products—relaxed, tanned, fresh, and gut-wrenchingly gorgeous.

'Good morning,' he said. 'I take it you slept well?'

Tamsin sat bolt upright and pushed her hair back from her face. 'No, I didn't, I—' she spluttered in protest. 'I wasn't asleep. I've been working! That was just—'

'Another power nap?' he said, with mocking gravity. 'Of course. Anyway, you'll be pleased to know that we'll be landing in a few minutes.'

She would have liked nothing more than a shower and a change of clothes, but there was no time, so had to content herself with brushing her teeth and splashing her face with water in the tiny but opulent shower room, emerging just in time to fasten her seatbelt as the plane came in to land.

It touched down with a bump and came to a standstill on the tarmac. Tamsin felt desperately impatient to be out of the confined space, and she watched as the ground crew placed the steps alongside. Alejandro didn't seem to be in any hurry, hardly glancing up from his coffee as the door was thrown open.

Tamsin gave a small gasp.

Two uniformed men appeared at the top of the steps and came into the body of the plane. In the sunlight from the open door, she caught the dull gleam of guns at their belts as they spoke in low, rapid Spanish to Alberto.

'Alejandro!' she croaked, instinctively moving towards him and reaching out to touch his arm. Her heart was hammering and her skin felt suddenly clammy. There seemed to be an iron band around her chest, making it difficult to breathe. Beside her Alejandro felt very strong and very safe. 'Alejandro—look.'

'Hmm? Is something wrong?'

'They have guns.'

Slowly Alejandro raised his head. His expression of total impassivity didn't flicker as he looked across at the men, but surreptitiously he reached to unfasten his seatbelt.

'Don't make any sudden moves, and do exactly as I say,' he said very quietly.

Swallowing hard, Tamsin nodded, desperately trying to resist the urge to throw herself into the safety of his arms. He leaned closer to her to whisper into her ear, and she closed her eyes, focusing on his voice, knowing absolutely that if anyone could protect her, it would be him.

'You can start by getting out your passport,' he breathed.

Her eyes flew open, and her gasp of fury and outrage was lost as the two uniformed men spotted Alejandro and came forward with jovial cries of welcome, uttered in exuberant Spanish. While they greeted each other in a flurry of handshaking and back-slapping, Tamsin gritted her teeth and waited for the burning in her cheeks to subside as it dawned on her that these were customs officials.

This was no ordinary plane, and Alejandro D'Arienzo was clearly no ordinary passenger here. There was no queuing to get through customs for him. Here the mountain came to Mohammed.

As Alejandro spoke to the men in rapid Spanish, Tamsin listened in fascination to the rise and fall of his low, musical voice. This was the language he had been born to speak, she thought distractedly. It was like suddenly seeing a beautiful piece of art in its proper setting. He had always spoken perfect English, so that anyone hearing him would never guess that he had neither heard nor uttered a word of the language for the first five years of his life, but there was a slight stiffness in his speech. A formality that contributed to his aura of distance.

Not so now when he spoke Spanish. He came alive. His voice flowed across her like a caress. A promise. An invitation. She felt her stomach tighten and heat spread downwards through her as her imagination supplied fanciful meaning to the delicious-sounding words she couldn't understand.

And then suddenly she realised that they were all looking at her, and that one of the men, the swarthy, bearded one, was coming towards her. She stiffened, throwing back her head and looking questioningly at Alejandro as the man gave her a courteous nod of his head and made a gesture she didn't understand.

'What do they want?' she said warily.

'Relax. It's just a formality. They're from customs. They just want to give you a quick search.'

Tamsin felt her eyes widen in shock and fear as the bearded man advanced on her, and she found herself automatically moving towards Alejandro. 'Oh, for goodness' sake,' she hissed. 'What do I have to do?'

'This.'

He stood in front of her and lifted her arms. Then, keeping his face perfectly still, his hands came to rest lightly on her waist and he murmured, 'Good. Now, stand with your legs apart.'

A wave of liquid heat crashed through her. She looked up to find his eyes on hers, filled with smouldering amusement. The bearded customs official moved round so that he was standing behind her, and began skimming his hands over her.

His touch was completely professional, totally impersonal, but pinned beneath Alejandro's shimmering, golden gaze Tamsin felt like she was naked. She kept her chin held high, biting her lip to stop her breath from escaping her in ragged gasps of fury and humiliation as Alejandro looked at her, and kept on looking.

'Is this really necessary?' she said through clenched teeth, aware that nerves had made her voice take on a cut-glass haughtiness that was wholly unnatural. 'I'm hardly a drug-smuggling criminal.'

Alejandro's eyes darkened to the colour of rich honey, and she watched as his mouth curved into a smile of pure, mocking pleasure at her discomfiture as the customs officer's hands moved down her body, lightly touching her ribs beneath her breasts, grazing her waist, her hips. 'Unfortunately, they don't know that. Your title means nothing here, Lady Calthorpe. Nothing good, anyway,' he drawled, the husky gentleness of his tone belying the cruelty of his words. Tamsin's insides melted as her eyes blazed with defiance.

The customs man's hands were moving upwards again, lightly patting the outsides of her legs, her hips, her bottom...

He stopped, and said something in Spanish. Alejandro gave a curt nod.

'He'd like you to empty your back pockets, please.'

Oh, God.

No.

Tamsin felt the blood rush to her face in a shaming tide of crimson as panic gripped her by the throat and squeezed. 'What? I've got nothing—why should I?'

Alejandro's voice was like velvet now. 'Your pockets.'

Setting her chin and lifting her head, Tamsin moved her hand to the back pocket of her jeans. Alejandro watched her with the intensity of a lion watching a deer, his eyes glittering with an emotion Tamsin couldn't and didn't want to interpret.

At that moment she didn't want to do anything except vanish in a puff of smoke. Or be kidnapped by aliens.

Her fingers fumbled for the back pocket of her jeans.

About now would be good—*just before she had to pull out a handful of condoms in front of Argentine customs officials and Alejandro D'Arienzo.*

She held her hand out, and then looking defiantly at the customs man, uncurled her fist. Frowning, the man looked uncertainly at the foil packets lying on the palm of her upturned hand. Time seemed to hang suspended for a moment while he picked one up and looked at it.

His shout of laughter echoed through the body of the small plane. Clutching his sides with mirth, he turned round and showed the other guard, who joined in the hilarity.

Smoothing back her hair, composing her face into an expression of haughty resignation, Tamsin's gaze flickered across to Alejandro's face as she steeled herself against the blistering mockery she expected to see there too.

Her heart stopped and her throat tightened as she saw that it was as cold and hard as marble.

CHAPTER EIGHT

AND that was what you called being caught red-handed.

Red-handed and red-cheeked, Alejandro thought contemptuously as he recalled the colour that had risen into her upturned, defiant face as she'd stood there with her outstretched hand full of condoms before shoving them back into the pocket she'd taken them from. She'd said nothing, probably because she was intelligent enough to realise that even she, Tamsin Calthorpe, who always managed to flirt and charm her way out of any awkward situation, had backed herself right into a corner this time. It was exactly that habit of seducing herself out of trouble that had just been exposed.

Because it was embarrassingly obvious that that was exactly what she'd intended to do. She'd clearly planned on using every trick in the book so that by the time they landed in Argentina he would be eating out of her hand, and the whole inconvenient business of the job she was supposed to be doing would be forgotten.

Her confidence in her own powers of seduction was quite breathtaking. Alejandro wondered how many men had fallen for it.

Tapping one finger irritably against the walnut inlay of the car door, he stared unseeingly out of the window at the familiar, flat landscape of the Argentine pampas. Usually his heart lifted whenever he travelled this stretch of road towards San Silvana, which was the only place that had ever felt like home, the only place he could ever relax. But now, with Tamsin Calthorpe sitting beside him, the possibility of being able to relax seemed as remote as walking on the moon.

The chauffeur swung the car smoothly between the tall gate-posts of San Silvana, and Alejandro caught his first glimpse of the house in the distance through the avenue of eucalyptus trees. At least, unlike the close confinement of the plane, San Silvana was big enough so that they wouldn't be on top of each other.

Unfortunate turn of phrase.

'That's where you live?'

Her voice interrupted his thoughts, and he turned to look at her. She was leaning forward, craning her head to see the building that was still tantalisingly screened by the canopy of the trees, and for a moment he was caught offguard by the sweetness of her profile, with its small, slightly upturned nose and her softly bowed lips.

He gave a brusque nod. 'Welcome to San Silvana.'

'It's pretty impressive.' She was trying to sound nonchalant, but Alejandro picked up the hint of irritation behind the words. He felt a momentary spark of satisfaction. What had she expected—some primitive shack with a corrugated-iron roof and a tin bath?

'Civilisation has spread to this far-flung corner of the globe, you know,' he said dryly. 'Did you think that gracious living didn't extend beyond English shores?'

'Of course not,' she snapped. 'I'm just intrigued, that's all.'

'By how I came to own it?' he demanded.

'Well…' Once again, a rose-pink blush was creeping up into her cheeks. 'You did say that you'd come from nothing, and that you'd worked for everything you have,' she said crossly. 'So what exactly do you *do* for a living?'

'I'm in business.'

They rounded the last corner of the sweeping drive, and Tamsin lowered the window and leaned her head out, both to get a better look at the house and escape his maddening scrutiny. The heat closed around her like a blanket as up ahead the house came properly into view. Built at the end of the nineteenth century in Spanish style, San Silvana rose up from the flat plains of the Argentine pampas like an ornate wedding cake.

When Alejandro had told her that he lived on an *estancia* she had imagined something rustic and low key, a comfortable old farmhouse or something. This fairy-tale palace was just one more shock to deal with.

She wasn't sure that her very hasty packing was going to be adequate.

'What business?' she muttered. 'International arms dealing? Opium farming?'

'I buy companies. Businesses that are struggling or facing liquidation. If they're worth saving, I invest in them and get them back on their feet. If they're not, I strip them down and sell off the assets.'

He spoke with a clinical detachment that sent a shiver down Tamsin's spine and brought back the cold feeling inside her chest, like she was choking on an ice cube. She thought of the pile of bills at home that she hadn't been able to face opening.

'Nice,' she said bleakly.

'Not always. But life in the real world isn't always *nice*.'

He didn't bother to keep the stinging disdain from his voice. The car came to a standstill in front of the house, and Tamsin fumbled with her seatbelt, keeping her head bent so he couldn't see her face. He obviously assumed a girl like her would know nothing about the harsh realities of business.

If only.

'I know that, thank you very much,' she said with admirable calm as the driver opened her door and stood back. 'But it doesn't make it any easier if you're the one whose assets are being stripped down and sold off. Of course, I don't suppose any of that matters to you.' She got out of the car and looked pointedly up at the majestic white frontage of the house. 'Profit is obviously what counts.'

He didn't reply. *Couldn't* reply, she thought smugly, crossing her arms. He clearly couldn't think of any smart way of ducking out of that one, when the evidence was right in front of them both. Keen to press home her advantage, she carried on.

'Of course, I don't suppose it would occur to you that behind every business failure there's a whole lot of heartache. Broken dreams can't have a price slapped onto them and be sold on, you know.'

Still no answer, eh? She'd really got him there. Turning round with a superior smile, she prepared herself to face the hostility that would tell her he knew she was right.

But he wasn't there. The driver was unloading their baggage from the back of the car, but there was no sign of Alejandro at all. Giving a gasp of outrage, she looked around, and saw his broad, retreating back just about to disappear around the other side of the house.

'Alejandro!'

Stamping her foot in frustration, she watched him stop and turn round, shading his eyes against the sun as he looked back at her.

'Yes?'

His voice was totally flat, utterly indifferent to the fact that he'd just brought her halfway around the globe and abandoned her on the doorstep. She opened her mouth, but, at the sight of him standing in his faded jeans and soft white T-shirt, with the sun turning his skin to burnished bronze, she felt the words die in her dry throat. Suddenly she wasn't angry any more. She was just tired. And lonely. And unsure.

'What do I do now?' she croaked.

He didn't hear. Dropping his hand, he was already starting to turn and carry on in the direction he'd been taking. 'Just go in,' he called over his shoulder. 'Giselle will show you to your room.'

'Giselle?'

'My PA. She's on her way.'

He was almost at the corner of the house now. 'Where are you going?' Tamsin shouted, wincing at the blatant neediness in her voice.

'It's the polo season,' he said simply. 'I'm going to the stables.'

The stables.

OK, well that was one place he was quite safe, because there was no way Tamsin was going near any horses. Which left her little choice but to do as he'd said.

Wearily she climbed the stone steps to the front of the house. Ahead of her the double doors were thrown open against the sticky heat of the day, and the interior of the house looked cool and dim. She peered into the gloom for this Giselle, preparing herself to confront some glossy super-model type with melting brown eyes and hair like oiled mahogany. Tentatively she pulled an iron bell-pull, wincing slightly as she heard its ring echoing through the silent house in the distance, but almost immediately a door opened and rapid footsteps clattered across the polished wooden floor towards her.

'*Hola!* Forgive me, Señorita Calthorpe, how terrible that you are left to find your own way in. Come in, come in!'

Tamsin smiled as relief crashed through her. The woman who came bustling towards her was in her sixties at least, short and comfortably rounded with a faded rose-patterned apron covering her ample bosom, and her grey hair swept up into a magnificent arrangement on the top of her head. 'Oh, please, don't worry. You must be Giselle?'

The woman gave a snort of disdain and rolled her eyes. She opened her mouth to speak but was at that moment interrupted by a cool, husky voice from the doorway behind them.

'Thank you, Rosa, I'll look after Lady Calthorpe now.'

Tamsin's heart sank as the sultry Latin beauty from her tortured fantasy stepped elegantly out of her imagination and into real life, swaying seductively across the faded silk-rug on impossibly sexy four-inch heels. She held out a slender, scarlet-tipped hand as her lips spread into a smile that didn't reach her eyes.

'Lady Calthorpe. I'm Giselle, Alejandro's personal assistant.'

Whatever her other talents—and Tamsin could quite easily imagine—it became clear as Giselle led her through the spacious rooms and wide, high-ceilinged corridors of the beautiful house that Alejandro hadn't hired his PA for her skill in making small talk or putting people at ease. Even walking three paces ahead of Tamsin at all times, and speaking only when absolutely necessary, she still managed to emit signals of unmistakable unwelcome. At least with Giselle on his staff he wouldn't need a guard dog, Tamsin thought sourly.

Finally they came to a suite of offices at the back of the house. She followed Giselle into a room that was long and sunny, with glorious views out onto the kind of lush garden that people back in England paid to visit. The room was furnished in a simple, modern style, which contrasted with the heavy grandeur of the rest of the house, and at one end a large, square fabric-cutting table had been set up, alongside a desk complete with state-of-the art computer equipment and a sewing machine.

'This is where you will work,' Giselle said, flicking her curtain of dark hair over her shoulder. Looking around, Tamsin gave a slow nod of approval. It certainly compared pretty favourably with her scruffy studio above the tattoo parlour in Soho where the England strip had been created. But then she spotted the other desk. The one in front of the heavy mahogany door to an adjoining room.

'And this desk?'

'Is mine.' Giselle gave Tamsin a smile that reminded her of an alligator—languid, but dangerous.

'How cosy,' said Tamsin, with only the barest hint of sarcasm. Obviously Alejandro had instructed Giselle to keep an eye on her, and make sure that she wasn't going to import a busload of 'proper' designers the moment his back was turned. 'Where is Alejandro's office?'

In a gesture that managed to be both indolent but distinctly proprietorial, Giselle waved her manicured hand in the direction of the door behind her desk. 'There. If you'd like to see him, just ask,' she said loftily.

'Thank you,' said Tamsin, smiling through gritted teeth.

It would be a cold day in hell before that happened.

'So, it sounds like you've got the kit design in hand, but how's it going otherwise? D'Arienzo's place is supposed to be quite something.'

Tamsin hesitated and looked out over the rolling sweep of emerald lawn to the wide, open plain of the pampas beyond. Steve Phillips was the production manager of the sportswear company who'd manufactured the England kit, and she'd got to know him pretty well in the months that they'd worked together. The Great Shirt Disaster had certainly been a very bonding experience, but, even so, she didn't know him well enough to answer his question honestly.

'It is,' she said bravely. 'The weather's gorgeous, and I've spent the last couple of days working on my laptop in the garden under a massive tree. It sure beats being in a stuffy old studio any day.'

At the other end of the line she could hear groans of envy as Steve relayed her message to the rest of the office. Imagining them all amidst the chaos of fabric samples and coffee mugs, with the traffic roaring past on the rainy Archway Road outside, sent a wave of homesickness crashing through her.

If only they knew, she thought bleakly as she said goodbye and hung up. San Silvana might be heaven on earth, but even paradise could get pretty lonely when the only other people in it hated your guts.

It was a relief that in the three days since they'd arrived she hadn't seen Alejandro at all, but what bothered her was the sour, churning certainty that Giselle was seeing him all the time.

She'd managed just one tense morning in their shared office before it had all got too much. Giselle's blank hostility was bad enough, but Tamsin could deal with that. No, it was the sudden warmth and animation she showed when she was on the phone to Alejandro that had really got on Tamsin's nerves. Watching for the third time as Giselle had rotated languidly on her leather office-chair, swinging one long, slim leg and curling a strand of dark hair around her finger as she'd spoken into the receiver in low, husky Spanish, Tamsin had realised that she would never finish the commission if she stayed working there. Mainly because she would end up throwing her laptop at Giselle's head.

Taking her things and venturing outside, she'd found this shady spot under a huge, spreading cedar tree and had set up a makeshift office. From here, for the last two days she'd been liaising with the manufacturers in London, as well as cleaning up and finalising the four designs she'd come up with on the plane, until they were all at a stage she was happy with.

But despite the fact the work was going smoothly she felt miserable and on edge. The feeling reminded her of when she was a child, after she'd had the accident. She remembered being terribly anxious for a while, secretly and shamefully afraid of hurting herself again, quietly trying to avoid situations that seemed even remotely unsafe. That was how she felt again now, only it wasn't her elbow she was trying to protect. It was her heart.

Suddenly she became aware of a sound in the distance that made the hairs stand up on the back of her neck and hot needles of fear prickle all over her scalp. For a moment she thought she was imagining it, that thinking about the accident had brought it all back, but the unmistakable sound of hoofbeats grew louder and closer. Desperately she scrambled to her feet and moved around to the other side of the tree as a refuge.

The horse appeared from behind a thicket of shrubs about twenty metres away. Relief burst inside her as she saw that there was a rider on its back—someone who would be able to make it stop or keep it well away from her. Leaning against the rough trunk of the massive cedar tree for support, she waited for it to pass.

It was galloping, but there was something almost leisurely about its pace, giving the impression of plenty more power waiting to be unleashed from its glossy, muscular quarters. And then her heart seemed to stop altogether as she realised with a jolt of agony and deep, primal recognition that the rider was Alejandro.

He was wearing knee-length boots over his jeans, but no hat. Even Tamsin, who knew nothing about these things, could see that he sat on the horse with natural grace and ease, so that the glossy, vibrant animal seemed to be almost like an extension of himself. Suddenly noticing her, he pulled the horse up so that it swung round on its hind legs like a ballerina. Tamsin felt faint with terror.

'So this is where you're hiding. I was about to send out a search party.'

'Hiding? I'm not hiding,' snapped Tamsin. And then, realising she was in fact cowering behind a tree, she stepped forward. Brushing imaginary dust off the front of her white linen shirt, she tried to keep the fear from showing on her face as she kept one wary eye on the stamping, sweating horse. The other was all too easily diverted by the sight of Alejandro's long thigh, just about level with her gaze. Mesmerised, she saw the powerful muscles flex as he held the horse steady.

'Giselle says you haven't been in the office since the day before yesterday,' he said tersely. 'She was worried.'

Tamsin gave a sugary smile. 'Oh, how *sweet* of her. Do reassure her that I'm fine.'

For a moment his eyes seemed almost iridescent with anger, and Tamsin felt a sick lurch inside her as she wondered if she'd overstepped the mark.

'Maybe you could do that yourself when you get back to your desk and get on with some work.'

Taking a step forward, she crossed her arms in front of her, determined to hide her fear. 'I *am* working.'

'Out here?' With faint incredulity he looked at the laptop on the ground, obviously switched off, and the mobile phone and bottle of suncream beside it. 'Working on your tan, maybe.'

'No. Working on your designs,' she replied hotly. 'Not that

you seem to be very interested any more. I notice you're not exactly chained to your desk, either.'

The horse was twitching and dancing, tossing its head and rolling its eyes alarmingly. But none of that frightened her half as much as the lethal note in Alejandro's voice when he said, 'I don't have to answer to you, Tamsin.'

Her fingers tightened around her arms, the left hand instinctively cupping the right elbow. Her heart was pounding like a sledgehammer in her chest as she looked up at him.

'Implying that I have to answer to you?'

'Exactly.' At the lightest movement of Alejandro's legs the horse surged forward, he circled once around her. 'I think it's about time I had a look at what you've been working so hard on. I'll see you at seven o'clock tonight. At the pool house.'

CHAPTER NINE

EXPERT hands moved slowly, firmly, over Alejandro's aching back and stiff shoulders, smoothing out the taut muscles, pressing away the tension.

Or that was the idea.

Lying on his stomach in the low, bluish light of the steamroom, he shifted restlessly, moving his head to the other side where he could see the smooth curve of Madalena's pretty behind as she leaned over him, massaging his back with long, firm strokes.

The steam closed around him, seeping into his tight muscles. He needed this, he told himself grimly. The Barbarians rugby match had cost him a lot of time away from polo, and he'd spent the last three days in the saddle, working obsessively on his technique and getting to know the new horses ahead of tomorrow's match.

'You're very tense, *señor*,' Madalena said softly.

Making a huge effort, Alejandro flexed his fisted fingers and tried to relax, tried to focus his mind on the game. The new palomino was a dream to ride, and he was looking forward to trying her out tomorrow. She had an energy and a responsiveness that told him that whatever he asked of her she would give—quicker, better, more bravely than he would ever have expected. With her gleaming golden colouring and silver-blonde mane, she was also beautiful.

Now who did that remind him of?

'Please, you must try to relax, *señor*.'

Madalena's fingers pressed into his tense, aching shoulders and Alejandro gritted his teeth.

Mind on the game. Concentrate.

Tomorrow's game was an important one. San Silvana and La Maya were old rivals, and the eight players on the field would be some of Argentina's highest ranking and most respected, himself included. *That* was why he'd been practising for twelve hours at a stretch for the last three days. Of course it was. It was to ensure that they got back the title taken from them by La Maya last year, and had nothing at all to do with trying to avoid…

'That will be enough, Madalena,' he snapped, sitting up abruptly.

The masseuse stepped backwards in surprise, her oiled hands held out in front of her. 'But, Señor D'Arienzo, I've only just begun. There's a lot of tension in your lower back and your thighs—'

'I said *enough*.'

Skilled and professional though it was, tonight her touch did nothing but set his teeth on edge. There was no way he could endure the feel of her hands working down his body, over his heated skin, while his mind refused to concentrate on tactics for tomorrow's match, and instead insisted on returning to the same dangerous territory.

Tamsin bloody Calthorpe.

Madalena slipped quietly away and he threw himself down onto a mosaic-tiled bench, breathing in the dense, pine-and-lavender-scented steam. The heat seared down inside him, scouring his throat and lungs, and he ran a hand over his sweat-slicked face.

She really was incredible. He'd thought that at least she'd make some pretence of working on the commission, but Giselle had informed him that apart from a couple of hours on the first day she hadn't even seen Lady Calthorpe. This afternoon, seeing her sitting outside, it had become abundantly clear why. She could hardly get her London contacts to send through designs for her to pass off as her own with Giselle sitting only a few feet away, could she? No wonder she'd looked so terrified when he'd come across her. She'd even tried to hide.

He sighed, letting his head fall back onto the warm tiles, and staring into the clouds of steam that billowed and swirled in the subdued lighting. She'd be here any minute to show him what she'd supposedly been working on. Maybe then he'd be able to cut through the deception and the pretence and expose her once and for all for the fraud she was.

And after that he would deal with the other bit of unfinished business that lay between them like an unexploded bomb.

For six years he'd berated himself bitterly for letting lust overcome judgement that night. However, what was starting to bother him more was not what he'd done, but what he *hadn't* done. If he'd been carrying condoms, as he usually did, if he hadn't left her, if he'd had her then on the cool, stone bench, he wouldn't be so tortured now by what he'd missed out on.

Back then he'd been punished for a sin he hadn't even had the chance to commit, he mused darkly. And, since he'd already paid the price, wasn't it only fair that now he got to taste the fruit?

The sun was beginning to slide down a sky the colour of watermelon as Tamsin made her way down to the pool house, her laptop under her arm.

She was early by at least half an hour, but it was quite deliberate. She wanted to make sure she had the laptop set up and all the information ready to be accessed in a couple of clicks before Alejandro got there. She knew that, the moment he came within a couple of metres of her, efficiency, competence and clear-headed professionalism were likely to be the first casualties.

She couldn't afford to let that happen. Having just spent the last hour in her room trying on every single combination of all the clothes that she'd brought, her confidence was at a low enough ebb already, and it wouldn't take much to get her well and truly flustered now.

If only she'd brought her red Temperley dress. That always

made her feel strong and in control. Or the little lime-green shift that she'd designed herself for Coronet, with the tiny black cardigan that slipped over her shoulders…That would be perfect for a warm evening like this. Cool and slightly sassy, but still professional.

Grimly she looked down at the pink and gold Indian-silk tunic she'd finally chosen in desperation. Usually she wore it over jeans, but she'd decided that that would send out a message that was way too casual, so she'd left her legs bare. At least they were brown from three days outside, she thought bleakly, stepping into the cool gloom beneath some eucalyptus trees. It was unfortunate that she looked like she was dressed for the beach rather than a professional presentation, but that was his fault. If he hadn't been so…so…*there* while she'd been packing she might—

Tamsin started as a woman in a short white dress, like a nurse's uniform, appeared from behind the row of trees. She walked with a languid grace, her treacle-dark gaze barely flickering in Tamsin's direction as she murmured, *'Buenas tardes,'* and passed her, going back in the direction of the house.

She might not have felt so out of place here among all these beautiful women.

Although maybe she would. Maybe she was kidding herself that clothes and fashion and this season's colours made the slightest damned bit of difference, because underneath she just wasn't sexy enough. That was why he'd walked out on her six years ago, leaving her with her dress around her ankles and her pride in bleeding ribbons.

The pool house, like the rest of San Silvana, had an atmosphere of grand European colonialism. A tall, square building, with white pillars and arched cloisters, from a distance it looked like an ancient Spanish church, but as Tamsin drew closer she could see that the old building was combined with elements of startling modernity. One wall had been completely removed and replaced with sliding-glass panels, which opened out onto an area decked in smooth, dark wooden boards.

Tamsin put her computer down on the big, square table in the centre of the deck and sat down in front of it, stubbornly refusing to be impressed by the stunning surroundings.

Cool and professional, she thought, squinting down at the screen. Cool and professional, that was how she needed to play this. Briskly she clicked open the files containing the designs, and the technical specifications and rough costings for each, and checked that all the information was there. And then she checked again. And then she sat back, chewing on her lip and glancing at her watch.

Still twenty minutes to go before he arrived. Her stomach gave a nervous lurch that was neither cool nor professional and yet again her gaze flicked towards the house, looking for him. Maybe it had been a mistake to be so early after all. She'd be a nervous wreck by the time he finally showed up.

Pushing back her chair with a harsh, scraping sound, she stood up. Now that the rosy sun had slipped down below the trees it was much cooler, and, rubbing her arms through the thin silk of her dress, she strode crossly into the pool house. The cold; that was what it was. The sudden drop in temperature was responsible for the goosebumps on her skin, not nervous anticipation of his arrival.

Inside the building the swimming pool itself only took up about half of the space, with the rest of it being given over to a sunny seating area, where wicker armchairs arranged beside an old wooden bar-area gave an impression of colonial elegance. There was also a smaller spa-pool, and a wet area, where water cascaded down from a lion's head shower, and in the wall at the far end were two frosted-glass doors. Tamsin found herself walking towards them, as curiosity fought with cynical indifference, and won.

The first door opened into a changing room. Two huge antique-looking porcelain basins stood side by side beneath a big-carved wooden mirror, and a kingfisher-blue wrap hung on a hook on the wall beside them. Hesitantly she walked over and ran a hand down its slippery folds. It was made of exquisitely fine silk, which shimmered and changed colour beneath her reverential fingers as she held it, at one moment appearing blue, the next changing to dark, shiny green.

It was lovely.

She took a sharp step backwards, letting the fabric fall from her hand, and watching it slither back into its shiny, secretive folds. Oh yes, it was certainly lovely. And Giselle no doubt looked great in it. Stiffly, Tamsin turned and left the room, rubbing her hand down her thigh as if the sumptuous fabric had contaminated it.

She pulled open the second door.

Instantly she was enveloped in a warm billow of pine-scented steam that curled itself around her and drew her forward. The room in front of her was dark and cave-like, lit by tiny blue lights set into the tiled floor, and in the thick swirl of steam it felt like she was stepping into a cloud on a hot summer's night. She took a couple of steps forward, tipping her head back and inhaling deeply as the door swung shut and the warmth embraced her.

Oh, this was good.

This was more than good.

The vaguely astringent fragrance of pine and lavender soothed her frazzled nerves as the heat eased the tension from her rigid shoulders. Pushing both hands through her hair, she closed her eyes, tipped her head back and breathed in again. And out, with a low sigh of pleasure.

There was nothing to see but blue-lit whiteness, shifting and melting into the darkness beyond. Blindly, Tamsin moved backward, groping for the seats she guessed would run along the wall. Her fingers brushed something hard and warm, and for the briefest fraction of a second a frown passed across her forehead as she tried to make sense of what she was feeling. She moved the flat of her hand further downward…

She froze.

'What the…? *Oh, my*…!'

Then her heart, which seemed to have stopped for a few beats, went into painful overdrive as she felt a lazy hand caressing the back of her leg. 'No, please, don't feel you have to stop,' said the all-too-familiar drawl. 'That was just getting interesting.'

She should move. Of course she should. Away from the fingers that were tracing languorous circles of bliss on her thigh. Away from the sense of menace that was now enfolding her along with the steam. But…

'I had no idea you were here. I thought…'

She felt the back of Alejandro's hand brush her inner thigh. She heard him sigh softly and felt him lever himself upright. The movement caused the steam to eddy and whirl, enabling her to see him in the gloom.

Her breath hitched in her burning throat.

God, he was magnificent. Naked apart from a pair of dark swimming trunks, he was sitting with his head thrown back in an attitude of dangerous ease. His skin gleamed like burnished copper in the low, bluish light, and her eyes travelled automatically to the sun tattoo that blazed on his chest. The steam thickened again, like drawing a veil between them.

'If you've come for our meeting, you're early.'

Low-pitched and languid, his voice seemed to curl around her like the steam. She could still feel the sensation of his fingers on her skin, almost as if they'd left a pattern etched into her flesh, and had to force her mind back to what he was saying.

'I know. I came to prepare.'

The haze of steam made everything sound sensuous. Even her own voice, in the dark and quiet and the obliterating mist, sounded husky and intimate.

He laughed softly, and the sound was like a kiss. 'Of course. I should have guessed you would. I'm looking forward to the rest of your *presentation*. But…' Tamsin could detect a sinister edge to his honeyed voice that made her spine stiffen. 'I warn you, my expectations are high.'

'If you're trying to intimidate me, it won't work.'

'No? And yet you sound nervous.'

She heard him move, sensed him coming towards her. Her body was hot and damp, the silk of her tunic was clinging to it like a second skin, but as he got closer she felt another, secret surge of moisture inside her. Desperately hoping for nonchalance, she let her head fall back against the wall she was leaning against and raised her knee, placing her foot flat against the wall.

'Nervous?' she said carelessly, 'Not in the slightest. Why would I be—?'

She broke off with a gasp as she felt his hand slip beneath her damp dress, against her heart. Her treacherous, thundering heart.

'You tell me.'

He was close enough now for her to see his smile and the dull, triumphant gleam in his eyes. 'Ah, but I forgot,' he went on quietly, his thumb very lightly stroking the sweat-beaded valley between her breasts. 'You can't, can you?'

Her whole body seemed to harden, throbbing in time to the painful beating of her heart beneath his hand. Her nipples were tight buds of concentrated longing. She wanted to move away but a terrible, silken languor had stolen over her, brought on by the caress of his voice and his gentle, insistent touch.

'You can't,' he breathed, 'Because honesty isn't exactly your strong point, is it, Tamsin?'

The words were like sharpened spurs on tender flesh. Pain tore through her, instantly bringing her back to her senses. Viciously she knocked his hand away and made to move past him to the door. But, with the lightning reactions that made him such a success on both the rugby pitch and the polo field, Alejandro reached out and grabbed her right wrist, pulling her back so she almost fell against him.

Tamsin went very still. Everything in her was telling her to pull back from him, but his grip on her wrist was like steel, and an instinct born of years of habit warned her not to make any sudden movement. Her arm was very slightly twisted, and bitter experience had taught her that it would take only the slightest movement now for the fragile set of the bones in her elbow to shatter again.

Slowly she tipped her head and met his gaze. His eyes were shadowed, impossible to read in the gloom. 'You know nothing about me,' she hissed, as adrenalin pulsed through her in waves and her breath came in shallow gasps. She frowned, desperately tensing her body against the urge to press itself against him.

'Wishful thinking, sweetheart,' he murmured.

And then—Tamsin wasn't sure afterwards how it had happened—some slight movement or change in their position caused red-hot daggers of agony to shoot up her arm. Momentarily distracted she went completely weak, falling against him as her lips parted to let out a small cry of shock, pain and misery. He let go of her wrist, his arms closing round her to support her, his mouth coming down on hers.

And she kissed him back. She didn't want to, but she could no longer hold back the tidal wave of annihilating desire crashing through her. Raising her hands, she gripped his face, feeling the stubble rasp against her palms as she slid her fingers into his damp, tangled hair. His skin was hot and wet.

Just like her. Just like she was.

The moist heat of the steamroom was nothing compared to the liquid fire that was building inside her as he stood in front of her, hard and strong and beautiful. His hands moved down from her waist, slipping beneath the flimsy fabric of her dress and then sliding up again, over the moist skin of her midriff, her ribs, up to her breasts. The high note of yearning that came from her mouth as he pushed down the lacy cups of her bra and her hard nipples brushed his palms was lost in his kiss.

His knee came between her legs and automatically she parted them, feeling herself pushing her hips downward, forward, against the rock-hardness of his thigh. Inside her head there was nothing but darkness and space.

And heat. So much heat.

Their mouths tore at each other, tongues clashing, probing,

retreating, in the same primitive rhythm as the movement of her hips. It was as old as time, and yet it was making Tamsin feel things that she'd never felt before.

Not since the first time.

The first and only time.

She jerked her head back, gasping for air as Alejandro's fingers dug into her waist.

'Alejandro…'

Darkness surged into the space behind her eyes, and before it overwhelmed her completely she made a lunge for the door, pulling it open and feeling the blissful rush of cool air wash over her feverish body. She took a couple of stumbling steps forward before she felt her knees give way and the roaring in her ears become thunderous, consuming her, sucking her down…

Alejandro caught her as she fell.

Bending to scoop her up, he gave a muffled curse. Desire still rampaged violently through him, and holding her lithe, pliant body against him was hardly helping. Her skin was hectically flushed, and her hair was dark gold with sweat, swept back from her face to show the angularity of her cheekbones.

Lust twisted painfully inside him, mixing with some other, less simple emotion.

Concern, he told himself scathingly. She was that English-rose type. He should have known she wouldn't be able to take the heat.

Striding over to the shower that was set into the wall, he turned it on full blast and stood beneath it, letting cold water cascade down, and taking the force of the powerful jets on his own shoulders so it ran onto her in gentle rivulets. As soon as the water touched her hot skin she stirred, opening her eyes and struggling to be released from his arms.

'Just wait,' he said harshly, his grip tightening around her.

'Let me *go*.'

He did as she said, and immediately she swayed and faltered, grabbing hold of him and coming to a standstill with her forehead against his chest. Glancing down at the back of her slender golden neck, Alejandro felt his sardonic 'I told you so' smile die on his lips as want kicked him viciously in the ribs. He just hoped she didn't look down or she'd find out exactly what havoc she was playing with his self-control.

He took her firmly by the shoulders and turned her round, so that the water was falling onto her back instead of his. And so that he was standing behind her. She made a murmur of protest.

'You overheated,' he said tonelessly. 'You need to cool down. Just stand there.'

She nodded, and he watched the water trickling down the back of her neck, making shimmering trails on her apricot skin. For long minutes he held her, until she stiffened and stood properly upright, and he released her.

'Sorry,' she mumbled, without turning round. 'I don't know what happened.'

'I do.' He turned off the shower, and as the splashing sound of the water died away the room suddenly seemed very quiet. 'You fainted in the heat. It seems that you can dish it out, Lady Calthorpe, but you just can't take it.'

She spun round, and Alejandro was surprised by the vehemence in her eyes. The pink-and-gold dress thing she was wearing was plastered to her body, so that her bra and pants were clearly visible underneath. Alejandro recognised the plain-white cotton underwear she'd thrown into her bag as she was packing, trying to make herself look so pure and virginal.

'Dish it out? Since when do I *dish it out*?'

She was shivering violently from the cold water now, and she spoke through teeth that were clenched to stop them chattering. The lips that had been so plump and reddened a moment ago had now taken on a bluish, bloodless tinge.

Without bothering to answer her, he strode over to take a towel from the pile on a rack near the shower and, throwing it over his shoulder, came back towards her.

'Take that wet thing off,' he said curtly.

With obvious effort she jerked up her head. 'Oh, I will…' she said through the castanet rattle of her teeth. 'But if you think I'm doing it here, you're horribly mistaken.'

And, grabbing the towel from over his shoulder, she stalked off into the changing room.

CHAPTER TEN

COOL and professional?

Oh, please. What a joke.

With a low groan Tamsin looked at her reflection in the mirror above the twin basins. The pale face that stared back at her with the dark smudges of mascara beneath the eyes and her hair plastered so unbecomingly to her skull was awful enough, but much worse was the memory of the wanton creature who had writhed against Alejandro in the humid haze of the steamroom.

Oh, God, the embarrassment.

But the pleasure too. The forbidden, delicious pleasure of kissing him, of feeling his hard body against her, and of fooling herself for just a moment that everything was as simple and as right as it felt. That they were just a man and a woman drawn together by mutual attraction, and he wasn't playing cruel mind-games with her.

She closed her eyes and rested her forehead against the glass for a moment before turning on the tap and splashing her face with water, rubbing away the mascara smudges. That was what he was doing; she was certain. He had brought her here determined to prove that she was nothing but a clueless posh girl with not an ounce of talent, but maybe he was beginning to worry that he'd got it wrong. And that would never do, would it? she thought furiously, rubbing her face vigorously with a soft towel. Alejandro D'Arienzo would rather die before admitting he'd made a mistake. He'd rather *seduce* her. Even though he'd made it abundantly clear that he found her about as attractive as yesterday's breakfast, he'd still rather kiss her into a frenzy just to undermine her professionalism and give her the best chance of completely fluffing the presentation.

And he'd nearly succeeded.

Who knew how far she would have gone if she hadn't fainted?

Furiously she peeled the soaking top upwards over her head, hesitating for a second before taking her sodden underwear off too, and then towelling her body and her hair with hard, decisive strokes as anger set like cement around her bruised heart.

Finally she grabbed the kingfisher-blue robe and pulled it on. It felt like adding insult to injury to wear something that belonged to Giselle, but she hardly had a choice. It was either wear the robe or do this thing naked.

It felt like heaven against her bare, tingling skin, and in the mirror she noticed with a jolt of surprise how the colour made her green eyes seem almost aquamarine. Not that you'd notice when the rest of her looked such a mess: her hair was beginning to dry already, and without the help of a ton of styling products was as soft and floppy as a baby's. Her skin, in protest at being steamed alive then blasted with icy water, was now glowing like a nuclear disaster.

Wonderful, she thought acidly, belting the robe a little more tightly as she went to the door. She was a fashion designer about to give the presentation of her life, and she looked like a seaside landlady after a night on the gin. One day she was sure she would look back on this and laugh.

It just wouldn't be in this lifetime.

Alejandro heard the door open behind him as she came out of the changing room, but he kept on swimming, keeping his mind focused on the rhythm of his stroke. Reaching the far end of the pool, he twisted beneath the water and, breaking the surface again, saw her walking towards him.

His smooth, effortless passage through the water almost faltered.

The blue silk-robe she was wearing clung to her slight figure, and with her hair white-blonde and falling softly over her face, and her skin glowing like sun-kissed rose petals, there was a simplicity about her that sliced into some unguarded part of him.

He reached the other end of the pool and ducked beneath the water again. The silent green world beneath the surface brought sense flooding back. Clearly he hadn't been entirely immune to the temperature in the steamroom either, and was suffering from an overheated brain.

Tamsin Calthorpe, *simple*?

Yeah, right. In the same way that Cruella De Vil was a dog lover, maybe.

Out on the deck she bent over the laptop she'd left on the table, but Alejandro kept swimming, cutting through the water with clean, forceful strokes, putting off the moment when he'd have to get out and face all of this. His head, which up until now had been so preoccupied with outing her as a talentless heiress with an influential daddy, was now unwilling to actually confront the evidence he had waited so long to see.

He couldn't even begin to unravel the reasons behind that.

Hauling himself out of the pool, he reached for a towel and dried the water from his face. His jeans were lying on a teak steamer-chair in the corner and he reached for them, checking that she was out of sight before slipping out of his wet trunks and putting them on. Normally he wouldn't have bothered getting dressed again, but this wasn't normal. With the feel of her lips, her thighs, her breasts still imprinted on his body and his mind, he could hardly sit beside her—knowing that beneath that blue silk thing she was naked—in *swimming trunks*.

Taking a couple of bottles of chilled beer from the cooler in the bar, he went out onto the deck. The heat had gone, and an apricot-tinted moon now hung like a jewel low in the pink sky. Tamsin glanced up as he put the beer in front of her.

'Thanks,' she said neutrally. 'I hope Giselle won't mind me borrowing this? It was all I could find.'

Alejandro let his gaze wander over the robe. Over her body *in* the robe. 'How do you know it's Giselle's?'

She looked up again, surprised. 'Well, I just assumed…'

Alejandro took a mouthful of beer. 'You assumed wrong.'

Two small creases appeared between her fine eyebrows, and she looked at him suspiciously. 'Then who?'

He shrugged. 'I don't remember. But, since I undoubtedly paid for it, don't worry about it. Now, shall we start?'

'Yes. Yes, of course.'

That's it; look at the screen, Tamsin. Open the file. Ye-es, that would be the one marked 'Los Pumas'…

Scowling with concentration, Tamsin attempted to force her shaking fingers to operate the laptop's irritating touch-cursor pad, swearing softly under her breath as the tiny flashing hand flailed wildly across the screen. '*I don't remember*'? *How many women did this guy have?*

'I'll start with the design that I think works best,' she heard herself saying as she brought it up on screen, and was surprised at the steadiness of her voice. He was standing behind her chair, and even though she couldn't see him she was painfully aware of the nearness of his broad, brown chest as he bent slightly to look at the screen.

She glanced up. The rose-tinted evening light made the skin on his hard, high cheekbones gleam like polished copper. As they flickered over the image his eyes were hooded, dark and unreadable.

'OK,' he said tersely. 'Next.'

That was it. Her best design, dismissed in one curt word.

'This one is more traditional.' She was aware that the effort of keeping the tremor from her voice was making it sound cold and hard. 'The colours of the Argentine flag are—'

'I can see. Next.'

Bastard.

Nervousness was beginning to give way to anger. Why did he have to be so rude? The third design appeared on the screen. Tamsin took a deep breath.

'You'll notice that the front of the shirts in each design has a space left somewhere for the sponsor's name.'

'Yes. Next.'

Her finger hovered over the file, but she didn't click to open it. Had no one ever told Alejandro D'Arienzo that if you wanted something you had to ask nicely?

'Do you have any idea who the main sponsor might be yet? Only it can have a surprising impact on the rest of the design if the company name has a particular font that has to be used, or a specific colour that their brand relies on.'

'That's something that the board are still in negotiation over. We won't know for some time yet,' he said with barely concealed impatience. 'Now, can I see the rest of the designs?'

Tamsin hesitated. 'There's only one more,' she said stiffly. He was towering over her. She could smell chlorine on his skin, but beneath that the bass note of his own warm scent vibrated in her head as she let the cursor hover over the file for her fourth design. Her throat felt dry as she clicked to open it.

This was the one she had designed with him in mind.

She took a deep breath. 'The shirts are designed to fit close to the body,' she said quickly, feeling her cheeks begin to burn. Her voice was a husky croak, and she paused, clearing her throat and slicking her tongue over her lips before continuing.

'In this one I moved away from having the traditional puma on the chest, and put the sun from the Argentine flag instead.'

Her heart was beating so hard she was certain he could hear its strong, primitive throb filling the dense twilight around them like a jungle drum. He came closer still, standing so that he was almost brushing her shoulder, and she could feel his warmth and hear the faint sigh of his breathing.

'On the flag the sun appears in the centre. You've put it to one side.'

Tamsin swallowed. 'Yes,' she whispered.

'Why?'

The single word was ground out through clenched teeth. For a moment Tamsin closed her eyes, willing herself to stay strong for just a bit longer. He hated the designs. He hated her. Things couldn't get any worse, which meant they had to get better soon, after this…didn't it?

Carefully she stood up, and tucked her chair under one table neatly before looking up at him. 'I did it for you. I was thinking of you.' And with her fingertips she very lightly touched the sun tattoo on his chest.

Alejandro felt his whole body go rigid at her touch, which was as soft and fleeting as the brush of a butterfly's wings. He was aware of a swell of emotion building up inside him, and concentrated on making sure his face didn't betray a flicker of what he was feeling inside.

His face, or his body.

So it was all her own work. No corporate-design team could have come up with something so personal. For a moment he couldn't speak as he watched her gather up her things, and bend down over the computer as she closed down the files, stroking her finger over the mouse-pad in a way that sent shivers across his skin. The light from the screen illuminated her face, and he noticed that the silk robe had fallen open slightly, revealing most of one small, lush breast.

He felt like he'd just taken a kick in the stomach from a fifteen-stone forward.

She folded the screen down with a click and picked it up.

'Perhaps now you'll believe that I am responsible for coming up with the designs, if only because you hate them all,' she said with a low note of irony in her voice. 'I'm sorry if you feel you've wasted your time bringing me over here, and obviously I'll arrange my own flight home as soon as possible.'

'No.'

The word had left his lips before he could stop it. He saw her freeze. Pausing, he thrust his hand through his hair as he fought to regain control. 'I don't hate it, and I haven't wasted my time,' he said very evenly. 'On the contrary. My plan was always to extend the commission, once the rugby designs were agreed. I'd like you to stay.'

Her mouth opened, but for a second she seemed to struggle to speak. 'Extend the commission?' she stammered eventually. 'Extend it to what?'

'Polo,' he said simply. 'Shirts for the San Silvana polo team.'

The warm twilight seemed suddenly to be heavy with invisible charge, like in the moments before a big storm. Tamsin shook her head, quickly, looking away from him and out over the garden to where the moon was climbing into a sky that was still streaked with fire from the slowly setting sun.

'I can't,' she said with quiet ferocity. 'I know nothing about polo.'

He gave an impatient shrug. 'So stay and find out. You can start tomorrow. There's a big match between San Silvana and La Maya, our biggest rivals. Come and watch.'

A shivering breeze briefly stirred the evening air, lifting her silken hair back from her face for a second before all was still again. A handful of tiny stars had appeared, and even they seemed to be poised, waiting for her to answer. She had half-turned to face him, the laptop clutched against her body like a shield, and he could see the indecision on her face. Complicated emotions clashed and warred inside him.

'OK. I'll do it.'

The tension Madalena had felt earlier in Alejandro's shoulders was instantly released. Managing to resist the urge to punch the air in triumph, he gave a curt nod of approval.

'Good.'

Quickly, as if she couldn't trust herself not to change her mind, she walked across the deck back towards the house, her eyes downcast. Alejandro watched her go, feeling frustration claw at his insides like a hungry beast as her robe fluttered open, giving him a glimpse of one slim, tanned leg as she hurried past him.

'Oh, and Tamsin?'

She swung slowly round to face him. Alejandro thrust a hand through his hair and kept his tone utterly nonchalant. 'After the polo, tomorrow night, there's a party at the club. You might find that useful to attend too.'

'*Useful*,' she repeated ruefully. 'Well, thank you. That's very… considerate of you.'

He scowled. 'So you'll come?'

'If it'll help my work, how can I refuse?'

What the hell had just happened back there?

Tamsin walked quickly, holding the laptop awkwardly against the slippery silk of the robe, and simultaneously trying to keep the front from opening up to reveal too much bare flesh, although the words 'stable door' and 'horse' seemed painfully relevant there.

She brushed that particular embarrassment aside. Showing a bit of leg seemed pretty irrelevant in view of the fact that she'd just agreed to stay on at San Silvana. Stay on and design *polo shirts* next, for crying out loud.

When it came to Alejandro D'Arienzo, she seemed to have some minor issues around saying the word 'no'.

For the sake of her mental health and her poor, foolish heart she really ought to be rushing back to her room to book herself on the first flight back to London and pack her bags. He liked her designs—whoopee—which meant that just as soon as she'd met with the Pumas' board and had a decision on a final design she'd be free to go. To get back to her business and her life.

Anguish gripped her, squeezing her insides as she realised the terrible truth behind those words.

What business, and what life?

Coronet was her life, and it was sinking fast. Sally had phoned earlier full of more doom and gloom. A rip-off of one of Coronet's signature dresses from the upcoming spring collection was already in the window of a high-street retailer on Oxford Street, she'd said. She'd sounded faintly accusing, like it was all Tamsin's fault.

This polo commission was not only a financial lifeline, it was a stay of execution, postponing the time when she would have to return to London and deal with it all. And postponing the time when she would have to leave Alejandro. Because, even when he was making her feel about two inches tall, she felt more alive in his presence than she ever had before.

And that, of course, was the real reason why she'd agreed to stay.

Her thoughts rushed onwards to tomorrow and what she'd just agreed to do, and she felt sweat break out between her shoulder blades at the prospect of spending an entire day that close to horses. Her elbow ached just thinking about it. And then, she thought with a rising sense of dread, once the horse part was over there was the party he had mentioned, which she could picture with horrifying clarity. Polo was the most exclusive, the most expensive of sports. What had she let herself in for?

But, more to the point, *what the hell was she going to wear*?

CHAPTER ELEVEN

THE printer clicked and whirred into life, spitting out a succession of pages which Alejandro removed from its jaws without looking up.

The cup of coffee that Rosa had brought him earlier was cold and untouched at his elbow, and the only light in the room came from the glow of his computer screen and the glacial light of the moon falling through the long, uncurtained windows. Flicking the switch of the brass desk-lamp beside him, the company report on Coronet London was thrown into sharp black-and-white relief before his tired eyes.

For the last few hours he'd scoured the Internet, tapped the few business contacts in London he knew well enough to call out of hours, and looked under every stone he could think of in his pursuit of information about Tamsin Calthorpe's company.

At the beginning he'd still been pretty sceptical. OK, so she'd come up with some interesting ideas for Los Pumas. He'd been surprised, he wasn't ashamed to admit it, but, having just browsed through endless paparazzi snaps of celebrities wearing Coronet on red carpets around the world, now he was a little less quick to dismiss her. Little Lady Calthorpe had set up quite a brand.

With a spasm of desire he remembered the grey dress she had worn at the post-match party; the way the gossamer-light fabric had hugged her body, the rather dramatic effect it had had on *his* body when she'd turned round and he'd seen the back.

All right, he couldn't deny it. Her clothes were good, so why was she losing money all over the place? Turnover looked healthy enough, and share prices were—

With a sudden sound of impatient self-disgust he threw down the report and stood up.

What was he doing?

This was the woman who'd lost him his job. The only question he should be asking himself about her business was why the hell he cared.

Tamsin took a deep breath and closed her eyes, wincing painfully as she made the first cut into the king-fisher blue silk. The sound of the scissors slicing through the fabric had an ominous resonance in the silence of the shadowy house.

She opened her eyes and looked down at the slash she had just made in the beautiful silk robe. Oh well, there was no going back now, she thought, cutting quickly up the line she had marked on the silk as she'd stood in front of the mirror earlier. It wasn't as if she had any choice, anyway, since she could hardly wear any of the stuff she'd brought with her, all of which would make her look like a Sunday school teacher at an orgy.

This was her best chance.

It was a long shot though. In her student days Tamsin had frequently raided second-hand shops and vintage markets for items to customise or remodel, but now the stakes were slightly higher. If she turned up at this glamorous event tomorrow looking like she was wearing something from a thrift shop, it wasn't only her personal pride that would suffer; Coronet's fate would be sealed.

The world beyond the pool of lamplight over the table faded as she snipped and pinned, working to some vague plan that existed only in her head. It was like alchemy. On the flat surface of the cutting table the fabric looked horribly raw, but she knew that it was important to keep going, to keep faith. Actually, it felt good to be working like this again. Sally handled most of the hands-on, cut-and-stitch practical side of the business while she did the designing, and she hadn't realised how much she'd missed it. Just the feel of the silk beneath her fingers was indescribably soothing.

It was very late and the big house was dark and silent around her as she slipped off the oversized white-linen shirt she wore over her bra and pants and gingerly stepped into her new creation. It was difficult to tell what it looked like with no mirror, but it *felt* pretty damned good.

Shutting the office door to keep in the noise, Tamsin stepped out of the dress again and sat down at the sewing machine. This was her favourite part: when the pins were replaced by stitches as a finished garment flowed from beneath her fingers.

The whirr of the machine seemed deafening in the moonlit quiet. Gritting her teeth, hoping that the house was big and solid enough to muffle the noise, she kept her head down and sewed on.

She was naked.

That was his first thought, before his eyes caught the narrow strap of a pale-pink bra across her back, and matching figure-hugging pants. Standing behind her at the door of his office, watching her bent over the sewing machine in the pool of lamplight, Alejandro felt the desire that had been beating a quiet, constant rhythm in accompaniment to his heart suddenly get louder, faster and a lot more insistent.

Testosterone, he thought dryly. Such a wonderful asset on the rugby pitch and the polo field, and yet such a pain in the backside in so many other situations. Especially when this girl was around.

'Your brief was to design the shirts, not make them.'

He barely raised his voice, but she seemed to sense his presence. Twisting round on her seat, her hands flew to her cheeks and then, as she realised that she was wearing next to nothing, to cover her chest. Making a quick lunge, she grabbed the white shirt that lay discarded on the floor by her chair and hastily shrugged it on.

'What are you doing here?'

'Working. You see, I do spend some time chained to my desk, although admittedly not during conventional office hours. More to the point, what are you doing?'

She glanced down at the puddle of blue silk in front of her, which shimmered like oil on water in the light of the lamp. 'Oh. This is for the party.' Their eyes met and she gave a faint, self-deprecating smile. 'Oddly enough, I didn't pack anything suitable to wear.'

The image of her standing in her bedroom with her arms full of clothes, that defiant, combative light in her eyes, came back to him. 'Of course not,' he said gravely. 'You didn't come here to enjoy yourself.'

She turned away, but not before he'd seen the pink blush stealing over her cheekbones, and he wondered if she was thinking of the steamroom. 'No. Well, I hope it's alright to…do this.'

'Be my guest. *Can* you do it?'

The light above the table in front of her shone through the fine linen of the shirt she had slipped on, so Alejandro had a clear view of the outline of her body. 'That remains to be seen,' she sighed. 'It's been a while since I made anything that didn't have to stand up to being grabbed in a scrum.'

'Given the behaviour of most polo players, and the way that these parties tend to end up, you might be wise to apply the same principles on that,' he drawled, trying to make light of the lust that was circulating through his veins like pure alcohol.

Maybe he'd been wrong to ask her to the party. Knowing her track record with the England rugby team, putting her in a room full of predatory polo players would be like letting an excited child loose in a theme park. She wouldn't know what—or who—to go on first. Crossing the room towards her, he felt the acid burn of primitive sexual jealousy as he wondered whose bedroom floor that dress would end up on in twenty-four hours' time.

'This is what you really do, though, isn't it?' he said abruptly, fingering the fluid blue silk and attempting to turn his mind, and the conversation, back to business. Her business, and why the hell it was in such trouble.

She didn't look up, hesitating before saying in a low voice, 'Yes.' The sewing machine started up again and he watched her slender, agile fingers guide the fabric through to the end of the seam. Then she stopped, and in the sudden silence gave a small, sarcastic laugh. 'It's what I used to do, anyway. I'm not sure there'll be much opportunity left to do it any more when I get back to London.'

'Why?'

'The business isn't going well.' Her head was bent, her silken fringe falling down over her face and hiding it from his view while her fingers went on working, deft and sure, finishing off the seam she'd just made. And then, so unexpectedly that for a second he thought he'd imagined it, a tear fell, glittering in the lamplight before sinking into the silk in her hands.

Emotion ripped through Alejandro like a flash-fire, a complicated mix of surprise, lust and a primitive urge to protect her. A primitive *ironic* urge, given how she'd screwed him over in the past.

She stood up, pressing her fingers to her cheeks, rubbing the tears away. 'Oh, God. Sorry,' she said with a gust of a laugh. 'How ridiculous. I never cry. Honestly, *never*. This is *so* stupid.' She backed away from him, swiping away the tears that kept falling with the heel of one hand as she bent to collect some scraps of material from the floor and gather sheets of paper together. Her movements were clumsy and uncoordinated, and a moment later she had knocked a box of pins onto the floor.

'Oh, sod it,' she moaned, dropping to her knees and trying to pick them up with shaking fingers. 'It's supposed to be lucky when you pick up a pin, isn't it?' She laughed bitterly. 'Maybe my fortunes will change now.'

'Perhaps I could help?'

'You're lucky enough already,' she muttered. 'Anyway, I can manage.'

'I wasn't talking about the pins.' Alejandro leaned down and took hold of her elbow. 'I meant help with your business.'

She went completely still for a moment, and then let him pull her to her feet. As she stood before him he could see the silvery tear marks on her flushed cheeks. Her eyes were the intense, glittering green of the garden after a sudden downpour.

'No. No. Absolutely not. Please, you mustn't think that's why I told you. It's fine. I'll sort it out myself, one way or another. I wouldn't dream of imposing my trivial business problems on you.'

The vehemence in her voice surprised him almost as much as her distress. He had got used to thinking of Tamsin Calthorpe as a girl who had nothing more serious to worry about than which designer handbag to buy next. It was taking some time to adjust to this new perspective on her.

'You'd hardly be imposing.' And from what he'd read the problems were hardly trivial, either. 'It is how I make my living, after all.'

'Oh, yes. I forgot. You buy up failing companies.' Trying to pull away from him, she gave a shaky laugh. 'You'll be stripping my assets before long.'

His grip on her elbow tightened. 'It won't come to that.'

'No?' She sounded angry now. 'Unfortunately, I don't have your confidence.'

Maybe not, but you do have a very rich father, said the cynical voice in his head. It cut through the cyclone of emotions, reducing them to an uneasy whisper in the back of his mind, but the lust that had been spitting and sizzling inside him for the last week was harder to dampen. She was looking up at him now, her eyes sparkling with angry tears, her cheeks flushed. Alejandro felt dizzy with want.

'Then let me help.'

Tamsin felt her resolve weaken. His voice was rough, but his gaze held her, and it felt like lying in a pool of sunlight. Strength, capability, total self-assurance radiated from him, and she wanted nothing more than to let herself sink into his arms, to let him take over, take everything on his broad, powerful shoulders.

'I…'

Unconsciously she relaxed the arm that he was holding, dropping it closer to her body so that his fingers touched her breast.

Her lips parted and a small gasp escaped her. It was barely audible, hardly more than a breath, but it was all it took to plunge them off the edge of the abyss around which they'd been circling since earlier.

His lips came down on hers, slowly, languidly. Heat exploded inside her as his tongue met hers and they began their erotic dance. His arms went round her, drawing her in close to his body so that she could feel his warmth and strength, and the hard, exciting pressure of his arousal through his clothes. His big hands were gentle on her back, and through the boneless, melting haze of desire she felt safe.

Safe?

What the hell was she thinking?

Who was she trying to fool?

With all her might she pushed against his chest, breaking free of the circle of his arms and stumbling backwards. She wasn't safe with this man. She was in more danger with him than with virtually any other man on the planet.

Alejandro D'Arienzo had the capacity to hurt her like no one else, and it would be the kind of hurt that would make the trauma of watching her business go under seem like a broken fingernail in comparison.

'Tamsin.' His low, fierce growl reached her as she ran for the door, biting down on her lip to stop herself crying out in anguish and confusion. She yanked open the door and ran into the dark corridor beyond.

In the darkness and moonlight everything was faded to ashes and pearl. Tamsin ran through the house on bare, soundless feet, thinking only of getting away from Alejandro, knowing that if she spent another second with him she'd crumble, and the silent battle that had raged between them since the moment she had faced him in the tunnel at Twickenham would be lost.

He had won anyway. All along she had maintained the struggle, but the most important victory had been his right from the start. Her heart had been his from the moment he'd first touched her six years ago. Before that, even, when she'd papered her bedroom walls with his pictures and kissed them every night before she'd gone to bed.

The game was lost. All she was fighting for now was her dignity and her pride.

From behind her in the gloom she heard a door open, and footsteps on the polished floor. Her pulse rocketed and adrenalin flooded every cell. He was coming after her. She let out a whimper of panic, looking around in desperation for somewhere to hide.

And what was that she'd just been telling herself about pride?

Quickly she ran across the hallway, making straight for the stairs. The moon was pouring molten silver through the high window beyond, lighting the staircase as brightly as a stage set. Tamsin's heart felt like it would burst out of her chest as she raced up the first few steps, but then she missed her footing and fell forward, knocking her shins painfully on the stair edge.

Two at a time, lithe as a panther, he was coming up the stairs towards her. With a gasping sob, Tamsin struggled to her feet, flattening herself against the wall as he approached.

'Are you alright?' His voice was like black ice.

'Yes,' she gasped.

'Good,' he said with sinister courtesy. 'Well, if you haven't got the excuse of any broken bones, perhaps you'd like to tell me what the hell you're playing at?'

'I'm not playing at anything,' she spat. 'We agreed. I'm here to work. That's as far as it goes.'

'I see. And since I've approved your designs there's no need for you to resort to any more of your seductive little business incentives?'

His words sliced into her like razor blades, cutting her so deeply that for a second she just felt numb. And then suffocating pain kicked in.

'No! You can't surely think that I would do that?'

Standing in front of her on the half-landing, with the moon-light falling on his huge, broad shoulders and silvering his dark hair, he'd turned into a statue. His physical perfection was like a taunt. 'What?' he said, and there was a hard, cruel note in his voice that she hadn't heard before. 'Use sex as a means to an end, to manipulate or betray? *Can't I?*'

'You *bastard,*' she breathed, stumbling to her feet. Her hands were balled into fists as she went towards him. Anger was closing her throat, making her feel like she was choking.

Alejandro turned round. His face was chilly and remote but his eyes glittered with malice. 'That's exactly how it looks from here, Tamsin, and, let's be honest, you do have previous form. Why else would you keep leading me on and then backing off?'

'Because I'm scared!' The words were out of her mouth before she could think, high and loud, a wail of anguish that echoed through the close night. 'I'm scared because I've never done this before with anyone except you, on the night you walked out on me!' He stood motionless before her, his face a silver mask in the moonlight. 'I'm a virgin, Alejandro. A pathetic, clueless virgin, with no more experience, no more seduction tricks or bedroom strategies to make things any less tedious than they were back then. *That's why!*'

He didn't move.

'Tamsin…' The word was a hoarse rasp. She carried on backing away, tears streaming silently down her face.

'Hilarious, isn't it? she laughed scornfully. 'Absolutely price-less. I'm so sorry for the embarrassment caused.'

And with that she pushed past him and ran up the stairs to her room.

This time he didn't try to follow her.

CHAPTER TWELVE

'SHE'S beautiful, Alejandro. Where on earth did you find her?'

Absent mindedly fastening his leather knee-pads over his white polo-breeches, Alejandro was about to reply, 'London,' when he realised that Francisco was referring to the new palomino mare.

He smiled wearily, ruefully, at his teammate. 'Palm Beach. She's very green, no match experience, but she feels like a natural and she's a joy to handle.'

He bent his head again, hiding his face and concentrating on buckling the leather straps as a wave of emotion smashed through him. He and Francisco were friends as well as teammates, but the near-telepathy they shared on the polo field meant that Francisco would be quick to pick up on any hint that Alejandro had something on his mind, and the last thing he wanted to do was have to explain about Tamsin.

Not when he didn't understand what the hell was going on himself.

He stood up, picking up his helmet as he walked grimly towards where the ponies waited, tied up in the shade of the tall trees that ringed the ground. The palomino mare was standing slightly apart from the others—old hands who were all languidly resting a bandaged leg in the heat and dozing with their eyes closed against the flies. As he approached he could see that the little palomino was tense and alert, quivering slightly.

She reminded him of Tamsin the night he'd met her, set apart from those other girls with their practised, confident charm.

He had got her so wrong, and now, somehow, he had to try to put things right.

He hadn't seen her this morning, but had sent Rosa up with coffee and a message that he would like her to accompany him and the grooms to the match and sit with them all in the pony lines to watch the game. It was a peace offering; a considerable concession. Before a match he usually made sure distractions were kept to a minimum, and apologising to a woman and talking about feelings had to qualify as a distraction of nightmare proportions.

No thank you, the reply had come back. She would prefer to watch from the stands and would make her own way there with his driver. And Alejandro had realised that not being able to talk to her, not being able to explain, was going to be a far more serious distraction all day.

Francisco and the other two team members were standing together in their emerald-green shirts, the colour of which represented the lushness of the San Silvana landscape. Alejandro joined them, knowing that as the captain it was up to him to summarise their tactics for each chukka in the match and say something suitably inspiring.

But now, like last night, words failed him.

Looking across the sunny ground, his eye was drawn to a figure in the stand. Amongst the diamond-draped glitz of the polo wives and girlfriends, Tamsin's understated beauty set her apart. Dark glasses covered the eyes that would have outshone the most dazzling emerald, and she was wearing a simple, pale-grey tunic top that covered her arms.

Alejandro felt his heart twist.

With Herculean effort he dragged his attention back to the three men in front of him and managed a grim smile.

'A lot rests on today. We have everything to fight for, everything to prove.'

* * *

Tamsin had never seen so many beautiful, glamorous, groomed women in one place. Sitting in the stands, surrounded on all sides by gleaming golden flesh bedecked in designer silks and diamonds as big as billiard balls, she felt as out of place as a dandelion in a bouquet of exotic blooms.

Not that it mattered. Bleakly she recalled the look on Alejandro's face last night when she'd spilled out the truth about herself. It wasn't just surprise, or even shock. It was total horror.

He hadn't even managed to say anything. This morning's invitation, sent via Rosa, definitely came under the heading 'too little, too late'. Even if it hadn't been for her pathological fear of horses, there was no way Tamsin would have accepted his patronising offer to join him and the grooms in travelling to the match. What was she, some awkward child to be appeased with a treat?

Shrinking further down in her seat, she tucked her knees up in front of her and opened her sketchbook, glad of the sunglasses that hid her reddened eyes.

It'll be fine, she told herself severely. All she had to do was get some idea what the game was about and how the kit had to perform. There were—what?—seven other players on the field. She didn't even have to look at…

Oh, God.

A sudden burst of applause signalled the arrival of the teams. Tamsin's fingers tightened convulsively on the pencil in her hand, jerking it against the page so that the lead broke as her gaze went straight to Alejandro. Instantly she felt the air whoosh from her lungs and her insides melt with scorching desire.

Shadowed by his black polo-helmet and a day's stubble, his face was as hard and grey as granite. In white breeches and leather boots, and a green San Silvana shirt with a number two on the back, he looked so impossibly sexy that Tamsin's throat went dry. He was astride the golden horse she'd seen him on yesterday, sitting in the saddle with an ease and insouciance that contrasted powerfully with the grim set of his face.

The two teams rode onto the field like warriors coming into

battle, their mallets held aloft against their shoulders like weapons. As they lined up in front of the stands, the atmosphere in the ground was electric, mirroring the palpable tension that crackled between the rival teams. But Tamsin was oblivious to everything and everyone but Alejandro.

The game got underway, and her aching heart felt like it had been ripped from her chest and thrown beneath the wild, thundering hooves of the horses. Never had she witnessed such violence. It was like a scene from Armageddon as the players pitched their galloping horses at each other so the animals clashed and reared, while all the time mallets sliced through the air and the ball ricocheted around like a missile. Transfixed with terror, Tamsin couldn't take her eyes off Alejandro as he streaked down the field, pursued by La Maya's number four. Despite their protective green bandages, the pale blonde legs of the San Silvana horse looked horribly delicate as she galloped for all she was worth, Alejandro bent low over her neck. Tamsin felt sick with fear as she watched the number four ride straight into his path, like a jousting knight. She felt the impact viscerally within herself as the horses clashed, throwing their heads up and wheeling round in a storm of flailing hooves.

How could the silken polo beauties around her watch this carnage so calmly? Were their smooth, impassive faces the result of genuine nonchalance or industrial quantities of Botox?

Just when she thought she couldn't take it any more, the umpire blew his whistle. It was like throwing a bucket of water over a group of fighting dogs; the two sides instantly separated, coming together at separate ends of the pitch in their own team colours. Tamsin breathed a shaky sigh of relief as her gaze followed Alejandro, unable to suppress the shiver of envy that rippled though her as she watched him stroke the pony's silken blonde neck. *Thank God,* she thought shakily. *Thank God he's alright, and thank God it's over.*

But a moment later she had to bite back a moan of dismay. The grooms were gathered at the edge of the field, each holding more ponies, and instead of dismounting Alejandro deftly slid from the back of the golden pony straight into the saddle of a mean-looking black one.

Tamsin turned to the expensively streaked blonde on her right. 'Excuse me? Is this half time?'

For a moment she thought the woman hadn't understood. Tamsin was about to repeat the question when she saw the beginnings of a smile lift the corners of her shiny red mouth. Slowly the woman slipped her diamant-encrusted designer shades down to the end of her very straight nose and looked at Tamsin curiously over the top of them.

'No. This is just the end of the first chukka.'

'Oh.' Tamsin's battered heart sank. 'And how many chukkas are there, again?'

This time the woman couldn't quite keep her amused, incredulous smile from breaking through. 'Six.'

Tamsin could have wept as she watched the players line up again for the game to restart. This time, on the black horse, Alejandro reminded her of a dark knight in some brutal medieval battle. She noticed how the other team members deferred to him, and how whenever he scored a goal the polo beauties lost their insouciance for a moment and the stands were filled with the glitter of a thousand diamonds as they raised their hands and applauded him.

Out on the pitch the sun gleamed on the muscular quarters of the ponies, now dark and shiny with sweat, as the battle raged on. Tamsin wanted to shut her eyes—behind her dark glasses no one would know—but she couldn't manage more than a couple of seconds before they flew open of their own accord again and desperately searched for Alejandro, making sure he was all right.

Why do I care? she asked herself in an agony of desolation.

The answer came straight into her head but did nothing to make her feel any better.

Because I love him.

* * *

Riding back to the pony lines at half time, Alejandro felt the black dogs of despair gathering around him like a pack of demonic foxhounds.

Against the odds he was playing well. Despite limited practice-time thanks to the Barbarians commitments, and a pretty much sleepless night last night thanks to Tamsin, he had scored eight goals.

If he could only keep his full attention on the game, he thought savagely, they might even stand a chance of winning.

But Tamsin's presence in the stands was like a thorn in his flesh. The first chukka hadn't been so bad; he'd been so blown away by the performance of the little palomino mare that he'd been mercifully oblivious to much else. But during the last two chukkas he'd been unable to shake off the awareness of her—so near, and yet so utterly unreachable. Her face was pale, half-hidden behind the dark glasses, and as he saw her drop her head into her hands it was impossible to tell whether she was caught up in the drama of the game or simply bored to death.

Hell, he needed to speak to her.

A crowd of autograph hunters waving huge photographs of him bought from the stands around the ground converged around his horse as he approached the pony lines. Alejandro was almost suffocated by the cloud of expensive perfume that engulfed him as he stopped to sign them. He gave in to one girl's request for a birthday kiss, but declined a rather emotional proposal of marriage from her friend who'd obviously over-indulged in the champagne tent at lunchtime, then quickly kicked the horse on, grateful that he had sixteen-hands-plus of rippling horseflesh between himself and the rapacious polo women.

Back in the pony lines he leapt lightly off the chestnut he was riding and, throwing the reins to a groom, went to find his mobile phone in the front of the horsebox. Shutting the door to keep the call private, he dialled Giselle.

'I need some phone numbers,' he said tersely.

The calls took longer than he'd thought, and when he emerged from the horsebox Francisco was waiting, his swarthy face creased with concern.

'Are you OK, my friend?'

'Fine.' Alejandro strode over to where the ponies were tied up, automatically going to the palomino mare first. The moment he touched her, her head jerked up. He could feel the tension in the bunched muscles beneath her satin coat; she was as taut as a bow string, but he knew that she was ready to go again, to keep giving, keep trying.

Just like—

'She's pretty special, huh?' Francisco's voice was gentle as it interrupted his thoughts.

Alejandro sighed, despair surging over him.

'Yes.'

It was only as Francisco gave the mare an affectionate slap on the neck that Alejandro realised he'd been talking about the horse.

Back on the field, the first thing he noticed was that Tamsin wasn't in her seat.

Get a grip, he thought furiously, galloping the mare round the perimeter boards, refusing to let himself look for her in the crowds of people coming back into the stands. But as the umpire threw the ball in for the start of the second half he couldn't help noticing her seat remained empty.

So she had been bored. So bored she didn't even stick around to watch the second half. Well, that was a first, he reflected, taking a vicious shot at goal. He was used to women eagerly taking whatever he offered, whether it was dinner invitations, gifts, or tickets for exclusive polo-matches. Given that Tamsin had just shown her utter disdain for one of the above, it didn't bode well for the peace offering he'd just ordered on the phone.

Applause broke out in the stands, telling him the ball had gone between the posts. Impaled on unfamiliar spears of fury and self-doubt, he was playing superbly, but for once it brought him no satisfaction. Unable to concentrate in the first half because of Tamsin's presence, Alejandro found her absence in the second half even more of a distraction. He played by pure instinct, and it almost came as a shock when the umpire blew the final whistle.

San Silvana had won the game, but, as Francisco galloped over to embrace him and slap his back, Alejandro felt no euphoria. He felt nothing but a cold suspicion he'd just lost something much more important.

Dejectedly Tamsin stood in front of the mirror in her room.

Well, that served her right, for getting side-tracked in the middle of cutting a pattern.

The kingfisher-coloured silk was as delicious as ever, but somehow she'd made the dress way too tight, so that instead of a subtle, figure-hugging wrapover style, she'd ended up with something that clung to her backside and plunged almost to the point of indecency at the front.

At least, now it was transformed into an evening dress, the robe was almost unrecognisable. Which was just as well, she thought bitterly, since there was every likelihood its previous owner would be at the party. She'd seen the women that had pressed around Alejandro at half time when she'd made her way over to tell him she was leaving. She hadn't bothered in the end. How pathetic of her to think he'd even notice she was gone.

She turned around, frowning at the way the iridescent silk shimmered over her bottom, making it look at least three times the size. 'Basic error,' she muttered gloomily at her reflection. She deserved to have her couture business go down the tubes if she didn't anticipate that tight fit plus shiny fabric equalled huge bottom.

She jumped as someone knocked loudly on the bedroom door, and hurried to open it. Giselle stood there, looking tall and willowy and so self-satisfied that it was obvious she'd never spent a single second worrying about the size of her bottom. Which was completely understandable, since it was as pert and perfect as the rest of her.

'Alejandro asked me to make sure you got this,' she said

coolly, her glance sliding curiously over Tamsin, and making the blue dress feel even tighter and shinier. 'He says he is…' She paused, seeming to weigh up the word. 'Sorry.'

'Thanks.' Tamsin reached out and snatched the stiff, shiny carrier bag Giselle proffered. Then, made ungracious by bottom envy, shut the door in her face.

Her heart was racing as she crossed the room to the bed, placing the sumptuous bag onto it. With shaking hands she pulled out the layers of tissue on top, finally reaching what lay beneath.

As her fingers closed around the silky fabric she felt her pulse go into overdrive. Slowly, wonderingly, she lifted it out, letting the fabric fall from her trembling hands.

It was as if the fairy godmother had just arrived and waved her wand, turning Cinderella's rags into the dress of her dreams. The emerald-green silk was as cool and fluid as water, falling in soft ruffles from the shoulders. Her professional eye traveled over it, admiring the exquisite cut, the originality of the design, while the rest of her swooned in an ecstasy of breathless delight at its sheer loveliness.

For about two seconds.

And then reality descended on her like an icy shower.

It was sleeveless.

Cinderella would be going to the ball in rags, after all.

There was a special kind of magic about the gardens of San Silvana at sunset. Usually, after a day in the office or out on the polo field, Alejandro found that going out onto the terrace with a drink in his hand, as the sun dipped down behind the fringe of trees by the pool house and cast long shadows over the lush grassland, was enough soothe the thorniest business problem or bitter match defeat.

But not tonight.

Ignoring the various comfortable chairs positioned around the paved terrace, he leaned against the stone balustrade and gazed restlessly out over the garden. He had waited for the opportunity to speak to Tamsin all day, but now his chance was almost here he was at a total loss as to what to say.

He had let her down last night; he knew that much. He should have told her straight away that her lack of experience made no difference at all. But that would have been a lie, and Alejandro D'Arienzo prided himself on always telling the truth.

The truth was, it *did* make a difference.

It changed everything.

He thought he was playing her at her own cold, ruthless game. Bedding her, on his terms this time, would be his victory.

So, yes, what she'd said changed things. He'd misjudged her, been wrong about her on every level, and now he felt he had to make appropriate amends. He had already set the ball in motion to help out with her business crisis, but the wrong he'd done her personally was less easy to put right. The dress he'd ordered was a peace offering, but it was utterly inadequate. What he really had to give her was respect, and that meant having the courtesy to keep his hands off her from now on.

'Drinking alone?'

He turned round. Tamsin was walking towards him across the terrace, and instantly the stiffness in his shoulders from today's match, and the ache in his back where he'd been hit by a La Maya mallet, faded into insignificance beside the twist of pain somewhere deep in his chest.

She wasn't wearing the dress he'd bought. The peace offering had been rejected.

Bitterness hardened inside him as he summoned an icily polite smile. 'Celebrating, if you'd care to join me?'

'You won? Congratulations,' she said lightly. 'I left at half time, so I didn't see your victory. Perhaps that means I forfeited my right to celebrate it too?'

'Not at all. Champagne?'

'Lovely.'

Rosa had left a bottle in the ice bucket, and as he tore off the foil he had a chance to look at her properly. If he hadn't seen her making it himself, he would never have recognised the plunging evening dress she was wearing as the robe she had found in the pool house last night. The transformation was incredible. Miraculous. She seemed to have sewn it so that it completely crossed over at the front, showcasing the smooth and perfect golden skin of her cleavage, gathering slightly on one hip, and then falling in a narrow column to the floor. When she moved it parted slightly on one side, showing an occasional flash of slender leg.

Gripping the bottle, he was just prising out the cork when she turned round and leaned her elbows on the balustrade, looking out over the garden as he had just done.

Lust exploded inside him like a plume of champagne foam.

Heaven help him. How was he supposed to keep his hands off her when her backside looked that good?

'Great dress,' he commented dryly.

She turned, her gaze meeting his across the space that separated them. The evening sun gave her skin a soft rosy glow that made him want to touch it. Or maybe that was nothing to do with the sun, he thought darkly.

'I'm sorry; I should have said thank you for the one you sent. It was lovely.'

He gave an impatient shrug. 'No need to be polite. If you didn't like it, it's hardly important.'

'I assume that Giselle chose it?'

'No,' he said shortly. Giselle had supplied the name and number of the boutique, but it had been he who had described Tamsin's shape, her size, and the extraordinary green of her eyes to the assistant on the phone. 'I did.'

'Oh.' She glanced at him from under dark lashes as he handed her a glass of champagne.

'But since it's hardly likely to be a regular occurrence there's no need to tell me where I went wrong. I don't pretend that fashion is one of my strong points. It was a long shot, just in case you had nothing else.'

Tamsin felt irritation, like an electrical charge, crackling through every sensitised nerve in her body. *I don't pretend that fashion is one of my strong points.* Meaning, presumably, that she did? That she did *pretend*? Suddenly she was glad to be wearing the too-tight, cobbled-together bathrobe dress, and that his exquisite silken caress had been folded up and put back in its bag. She would rather have walked naked through a pit of rattlesnakes than give him the satisfaction of admitting he'd got it right.

'Well,' she said sardonically, turning towards him with a small, determined smile. 'Here's to you. The winner. Again.' She held her glass up to his, and as the rims touched she saw the dark, closed expression on his face. 'It must get rather predictable, being successful at everything you do.'

'No. I never take anything for granted.'

He spoke tersely, moving away from her and draining half his glass in one mouthful. The tension between them, veiled by brittle courtesy, was like broken glass underfoot. *Why did I say yes to a drink?* Tamsin berated herself, remembering the girls who had flocked round him earlier. Here she was, delaying his arrival at the party by forcing him to make small talk, when clearly he just wanted to get away.

She took a huge gulp of champagne, turning her head away so he wouldn't see the dull blush that had spread across her cheeks. 'Sorry, I'm keeping you from the party.'

'No hurry,' he said coolly, watching her take another hefty swig of her drink. 'And, I think I'd better warn you, these parties can get a bit out of hand. Polo players are as passionate about women as they are about horses, so be careful.'

Hot adrenalin burst inside her, making her whole body fizz and sing with anger. 'Thank you for that, Alejandro,' she said through gritted teeth. 'But there's really no need for you to feel responsible for me. I might be a virgin, but I'm not a child. I have been to parties before, thank you very much. And anyway—' she tossed back the rest of her champagne '—I can't imagine I'll be in any danger of having my virtue compromised, since it's so completely offputting. Now, let's go, shall we?'

'Tamsin—'

But she was already at the door and she didn't stop.

It was obvious they had nothing to say.

CHAPTER THIRTEEN

A RED lace thong hung from one of the strings of fairy lights that lit the polo-club garden and, looking around, Tamsin spotted the matching bra draped over an azalea bush. From behind it came the distinctive sounds of passion in progress.

Alejandro had been right again, she thought sourly. Polo parties were pretty wild.

The scene before her was beautiful, but definitely debauched. The party was being held in a series of tents, which added to the historical atmosphere Tamsin had identified earlier. The overall effect was like some extravagant medieval pageant—from a distance, at least. The reality was less romantic. Rival polo teams lined up at the bars to compete with each other at downing shots, while couples were entwined together on the dancefloor in poses she'd only previously seen depicted in the Kama Sutra.

In the midst of it all Tamsin felt unutterably lonely.

She'd spent the whole evening focusing on avoiding Alejandro. The short journey had passed in complete silence, and from the moment they'd got out of the car she had made absolutely sure that she stayed as far away from him as possible.

This hadn't been difficult, since he was permanently surrounded by a crowd of glamorous people, all clamoring for his attention. The crowd was mainly composed of terrifyingly beautiful women who draped themselves around him like expensive accessories, but there were men there, too, other polo players who wanted to bask in a little of Alejandro's reflected glory. Tamsin was determined not to cramp his style, so had ended up talking to an endless stream of people she didn't know and with whom she had nothing in common.

Politely extricating herself from a rather one-sided conversation about diets with a pipe-cleaner-thin Brazilian model, she took refuge in the nearest tent. There was a bar set up in the middle where some kind of cocktail was being made.

'Ah…the elusive Lady Calthorpe,' said a warm voice close to her ear. 'Such a pleasure to meet you at last.'

She turned. In the dimness she could see little of the man who had spoken, apart from the gleam of his eyes and the flash of very white teeth in his swarthy face.

'I am Francisco. I play on the San Silvana team, alongside Alejandro. Let me get you a drink, *querida*, and then you can tell me all about yourself.'

He was back a moment later, handing her a shallow cocktail-glass and guiding her gently, his hand in the centre of her back, out into the softly lit garden.

'Do you mind if we sit down?' he asked, steering her towards a bench set into an arbour smothered with clematis. 'Today's game was pretty vicious, and I'm aching all over.'

Tamsin smiled. 'You mean polo isn't always that violent?'

Francisco laughed. 'It's rough, yes, but between La Maya and San Silvana it's more than that. It feels like a battle.'

'It looked like that too,' said Tamsin with a shudder. 'I was worried someone was going to get killed.'

'Someone in particular?' Francisco enquired gently.

Tamsin glanced at him sharply. In the light of the paper lanterns strung above them, his eyes were kind, and she could see the laughter lines fanning out from them, giving him an air of dissipated merriment. The urge to confide in him was too strong to resist.

'Yes,' she admitted bleakly, taking a sip of her drink. It tasted delicious, like melted chocolate. 'How did you guess? It's horribly predictable, and of course completely futile.'

'Predictable, maybe; Alejandro is an attractive man. But you are a beautiful girl, *querida*, so futile? I think not.'

'You're very kind, but unfortunately, even if I was in the same league as the women he surrounds himself with, I'm afraid that wouldn't be enough. There are other…issues.' She took another mouthful of her drink, and was surprised to find that the glass was empty. 'This is gorgeous. What is it?'

'Chocolate vodka. Is good, no?' Francisco laughed. 'I think perhaps in heaven they drink it all the time, but since I'm not sure I will be good enough to go there I have to drink it while I can. Wait here, I'll get us another one, and then you can tell me all about these other issues. Who knows, maybe I can help?'

The music pounding out of the disco tent had slowed to a more languid beat as Alejandro fought his way between the dancing couples that had spilled out onto the lawn. His progress was slow, as every few paces he kept being accosted by women en-twining themselves around him and asking him to dance. Some were remarkably hard to disentangle, and his efforts to do this were becoming less patient and gentle.

He had to find Tamsin.

All evening he had tried to stay near her, near enough to make sure that she was all right, but every time he came close she seemed to drift away again, so that the next time he looked she was nowhere to be seen. She had had no shortage of men hanging round her, he thought grimly, but, whereas a few days ago that would have filled him with contempt, now it made him feel fiercely protective. If any of them laid a finger on her…

'Hey, Eduardo!' Alejandro spotted the San Silvana number four coming towards him, his arms around a dark-haired girl in a silver dress. 'Have you seen Tamsin?'

Eduardo frowned. 'Blonde girl? Blue dress? Great back-side? Sure.'

Alejandro resisted the urge to flatten him. 'Where?'

'She was talking to Francisco over there, in a seat behind the vodka tent. But,' he warned jokingly, 'It looked pretty heavy, like they might not appreciate being disturbed. Hey—Alejandro! Alejandro, man! Take it easy!'

But it was too late. Pushing past him, Alejandro was already melting into the darkness, his expression murderous.

'To me, little one, the solution seems simple.' Francisco sighed theatrically. 'I cannot see why you say no.'

Tamsin picked up the hand he had placed on her thigh.

'It wouldn't work, Francisco,' she said with a regretful smile, holding his hand between both of hers. 'I know that he would find me much more attractive and exciting if I was more experienced, but the irony is that I don't want to get that experience with anyone but him.' She sighed. 'I think that's what you'd call a catch-twenty-two situation.'

Francisco stroked the back of his other hand along her cheek. 'Alejandro has always been something of an enigma. I have played polo alongside him for five years, and still I feel there are huge parts of his heart that I do not know.' In the darkness, Francisco's voice was suddenly serious. 'But never have I thought he was a fool, Tamsin. And, if he doesn't want a beautiful girl because she is not experienced, then that is exactly what he is.'

Tamsin closed her eyes for a second and took a deep breath of fragrant night air. The effect of the two chocolate vodkas was beginning to wear off now, and where half an hour ago she had felt elation she now felt only sadness. Francisco was so kind and so sympathetic; there was a tiny part of her that was telling her to do as he suggested. She could do a lot worse than being gently initiated into the art of sex by someone as sweet and experienced as he was. Someone uncomplicated, who would expect nothing she couldn't give in return.

And yet, of course, it was hopeless. The thought of sleeping with anyone but Alejandro was incomprehensible. It always had been. That was precisely why she was in her current situation.

She leaned forward, putting an arm around Francisco's shoulder and pressing a kiss on his cheek. For a long moment he held her. 'Thank you for listening,' she murmured. 'Just talking has—'

She didn't get any further. Suddenly Francisco was being yanked away from her and pulled to his feet by the open collar of his white dress-shirt. Tamsin gave a gasp of shock and terror as Alejandro towered above them in the darkness, his face a mask of rage.

Francisco wrenched himself free and for a moment the two men squared up to each other. 'What the hell do you think you're doing, feeding her vodka and feeling her up?' snarled Alejandro. 'Did you touch her? *Did* you?' His voice was a low, animal growl. Tamsin felt a cold wave of horror wash away the last lingering effects of the chocolate vodka as she saw that his hands were bunched into tight fists.

She leapt up, pushing between the two men. Adrenalin pulsed through her, icy and invigorating as she tipped her head back and faced Alejandro.

'You have no right to ask that question,' she hissed. 'I told you before that I'm perfectly capable of looking after myself. You couldn't have made it more clear that I'm nothing to you, so if Francisco—'

'Did—he—touch—you?'

Every precisely spoken word was edged with steel. His fingers bit into her shoulders, and his narrowed eyes glittered down at her from a face that was blank with fury.

Behind her Francisco spoke, his voice quiet and ironic. 'I think this primitive display of masculinity tells you what you wanted to know, Tamsin.' Gently he leaned forward and kissed her on the side of her cheek, before throwing Alejandro a warning glance and moving away.

Alejandro closed his eyes and let his head fall back for a fraction of a second. When he spoke again the blazing anger in his voice had died down to a white-hot glow.

'Did he?'

Tamsin held her head very straight. 'No. He *listened* to me.

He let me talk, and he listened to how I felt, and then he…' Her bravado faltered here, and she felt her throat constrict, making her voice crack. 'He offered to show me…to teach me… He was kind; he didn't pressure me; he just wanted to help.'

Alejandro's jaw was like iron as he put his hands to his head and shook it incredulously.

'God. My God, Tamsin… What did you say?'

She looked down. 'I said no.'

'Thank God for that,' he snarled, seizing her arm and dragging her forwards. 'Now, let's get out of here.'

'Why?' Tamsin stumbled, and he turned back to catch her, scooping her into his arms. 'Where are we going? Alejandro, what are you doing? I've told you, I'm not a child, and I'm not drunk, I'm perfectly able to—'

'Shut up,' he said in a voice like thunder, striding through the dark garden with her in his arms. 'I don't give a toss how old you are or what you're able to do. All I care about is getting you out of here and into my bed, because if anyone's going to show you anything, Tamsin, I want it to be me.' He swore quietly and succinctly. 'And, Lord, I want it to be soon.'

The moon had retreated like a shy bride behind her veils of cloud as they drove home, and the Argentine night was soft and dark. Alejandro made no move to touch her on the journey, and he was so silent and distant that Tamsin was certain that he must have changed his mind. When the moon peeped from behind the cloud, she glanced across at him and felt her insides constrict with excruciating need.

Feeling her eyes on him, he slowly turned to face her. His expression was terrifyingly bleak.

'Is this what you really want? You're sure?'

'Yes,' she whispered. 'It's all I've ever wanted.'

The hallway was completely silent. The moonlight made it look like a black-and-white photograph of itself a century ago. Time had stopped. The moment stretched and quivered as

Alejandro came towards her from the shadows, his face inscrutable, unreadable.

And then he touched her, cupping her cheek with one strong, rough hand.

Her swift, indrawn breath was a whisper of transparent longing in the intimate darkness. His thumb brushed her jaw, and Tamsin felt her lips parting in blissful, hopeful anticipation of his touch on her mouth.

She was trembling, quaking, with need and want and fear and ecstasy. Hot shafts of sensation crackled and juddered up through her pelvis, until it felt like she was going to split wide open with the strength of her longing.

He raised his other hand, and for a moment he cupped her face, holding her steady.

His voice was low and gritty. 'Come upstairs.'

She whimpered as he led her through the shadows, feeling her heart clench and twist as she caught a glimpse of his blank, perfect face as they crossed a bar of moonlight. Upstairs the blackness was more intense. Alejandro melted into the darkness in his black dinner suit, but his fingers laced between hers were warm and hard and real. He led her steadily, unhurriedly, so that by the time they reached the bedroom she was almost sobbing from fear and excitement.

Very slowly he took her over to the bed.

The curtains were drawn back from the windows, but the moon, from modesty, was round at the other side of the house and the light that came in here was a soft, smoky grey.

She heard him sigh, a lingering exhalation that touched her in deep, undreamed-of places. His fingertips skimmed her waist, her hips, the small of her back, and then he brought her very gently into his body, dropping his mouth to kiss the side of her neck

Spiked stars of pleasure exploded inside her like fireworks.

'Your dress,' he breathed against her ear. 'How do I take it off?'

Just the words were enough to drench her with creamy expectation. Her voice was little more than a moan as her fingers fumbled with the concealed button she had put where the dress gathered on one hip.

'Button. Here,' she rasped, pulling impatiently at the fabric so that she felt the stitching give.

Alejandro's hand was perfectly steady as it covered hers, his voice almost severe.

'I'll do it.'

She dropped her arms to her side as his strong fingers worked at the fastening.

'It's coming apart at the seams,' he said quietly, finally freeing the button and letting the silk fall away from one side.

Like me, thought Tamsin desperately as desire rampaged through her boneless, hungry body. Unravelling.

The other side was easier. Alejandro found the narrow satin ribbon and pulled it undone, so that Tamsin stood before him in her underwear. She was trembling violently. Alejandro's jaw ached with tension as he kept his teeth clenched together, biting back the moan of fierce pleasure that rose up in his throat as he looked at her. She was so perfect; he wanted nothing more than to crush her in his arms and kiss the breath from her body as he ravished her. But the effort of not rushing her, not frightening her, was monumental.

He had to take it slowly.

In a life of relentless physical challenge, this was going to be the toughest one yet.

His exhausted, battered body thrummed with urgency as, very gently, he pushed the silken robe off her shoulders so that it fell to the floor with a sound like a sigh. He sensed her tensing, and straight away saw her bow her head, her arms come up across her body, covering herself.

'You're beautiful,' he whispered, cursing himself for the note of hoarse desire that roughened the words. Resisting the urge to tear her arms away from their shield-like position in front of her, he dipped his head, barely brushing her collarbone with his lips, trailing them across the satin of her skin towards her neck, the hollow at the base of her throat, and upwards to where the pulse jumped beneath her ear.

Slowly, gradually, as his mouth finally found hers, he felt her arms slipping downwards, and the terrible trembling that shook her slender body subside. Alejandro felt dizzy with the effort of keeping his hands gentle as his head filled with the scent of her, the taste of her vanilla-ice-cream skin and chocolate kiss.

He wanted her so much. He couldn't hold out much longer.

Wrenching his mouth from hers for a moment, he pulled back the soft goosedown cover on the bed and lifted her up, laying her gently on the cool cotton sheets before shrugging off his jacket and kicking off his shoes. He didn't want to frighten or pressure her so he was going to leave the rest of his clothes on, but she rose up from the bed, and he felt her hands groping for the buttons of his shirt.

'Please. I want to see you, Alejandro.' She gave a muffled sob of longing. 'Oh, God, I want to *feel* you…'

Lust tore through him like a cyclone, shaking his noble intentions to their very foundations. He stood as still as a statue as she undid his shirt, and had to throw back his head and bite down on the insides of his cheeks to stop himself crying out a jagged shout of pure, devouring want when he felt her hands sliding across the bare skin of his chest, his shoulders, pushing the shirt off him.

The subdued glow of the moon turned her hair to silver and her skin to velvet. She was so pure and perfect, it almost felt like a violation to touch her. His hands felt too big, too coarse for such ethereal beauty, and he was grimly aware of the roughened skin of his palms. Gently he laid her back on the bed again, trailing the backs of his fingers down the length of her arms.

Tamsin stiffened, instinctively jerking her right arm away from him, but his steady, languid, expert touch didn't falter. He knelt over her, and in the soft, pearly light his face was as cool and remote as the moon, his eyes dark and secret like the unfathomable night sky. With his strong, sexy hands spanning her waist, he held her, then slowly lowered his head, and she gasped with joy and frustration as his mouth brushed one hip bone, then skimmed across the quivering hollow of her pelvis. His tongue circled round her navel, then very gently probed the dip of her belly button.

Oh, please, please, please...

Did she say the words aloud? Tamsin wasn't sure. Her head seemed to have been plundered, so that every thought, every naked, shameless desire, echoed through the throbbing darkness between them. She was still in her silken underwear, and Alejandro moved lower now, his hands still gripping her hips, holding her still and pulling the silk taut as his mouth closed over the place that hid the aching, pulsing core of her.

The silk of her knickers both veiled and heightened the sensation, diffusing the warmth as he breathed out against her. Tamsin was drifting on clouds of bliss, utterly deranged with desire, so that when his tongue slipped beneath the wet silk of her pants the ecstasy was indescribable. Bucking and wriggling her hips against his steadying hands, she screamed with joy and need.

Alejandro lifted his head. He had reached the limits of his endurance. Having her, feeling her around him, was now an imperative more urgent than breathing.

He had never wanted anyone, or anything, so much.

'Show me. Show me now, Alejandro.'

Breaking away from her long enough to kick off the rest of his clothes and grab a condom, he felt like he was coming home after some long and arduous race as he gathered her into his arms and their mouths met. She had slipped out of the silk knickers now, so only the little bra remained between them. Without letting his lips leave hers, Alejandro unhooked it with one steady hand, unable to suppress the ragged moan of greed that escaped him as her breasts spilled out against his chest.

And in the end he didn't have to show her anything. Easing into her with a gentleness that stretched his flayed nerves almost to breaking point, Alejandro barely even felt her stiffen before her legs wrapped around his waist and she was gripping him, arching up, and then, astonishingly, crying out in pure, abandoned pleasure.

Alejandro let go, his desire exploding with the force of a rocket in the night sky, shaking him, shattering him, and leaving him empty.

CHAPTER FOURTEEN

THE beat of Alejandro's heart filled her head and the Argentine sun on his chest was warm beneath her cheek as she lay there. Tamsin had never known such profound peace.

In the silvery darkness all was silent and still again. Gone was the roaring in her ears, the sound of thunderbolts and orchestras and fireworks that had echoed through her dazzled head a few moments before; gone was the scarlet whirlpool of ecstasy that had sucked her down. Now she was adrift on some warm tropical sea, rocked by gentle ripples of pleasure that still lapped through her blissed-out body.

Alejandro moved slightly, leaning away from her a little so he could look down into her face. He smoothed her hair from her forehead and held his palm against her cheek. In the half-light she could see him frowning.

'Are you alright? I didn't hurt you?'

She shook her head. The low, grave tone of his voice made her heart flip, and she didn't trust herself not to say something ridiculous, probably involving the word 'love'.

He sighed, and lay back again, pulling her against him. His hand moved downwards, lightly caressing her skin with gentle fingers. As he trailed them down her right arm she felt herself flinch automatically.

Instantly his fingers stilled. 'What's wrong?'

'Nothing,' she whispered. 'It's fine.'

He shifted position, so that he was propped up on one elbow beside her, and pulled her arm towards him. 'It's not fine. Let me see.'

'Don't.' Tamsin stiffened, trying to snatch it away, but his fingers were firm on her wrist as he straightened her arm and turned it over. Even in the dusky moonlight the mess of scars and stretched tendons was all too easy to see.

'Please, Alejandro,' she moaned. 'It's so ugly and horrible.' She had willingly opened up the most intimate part of herself to him only moments ago, but as he gazed down at her arm she felt truly naked and exposed. Her happiness ebbed away, leaving anxiety and shame.

'Of course it's not,' he said harshly, rubbing his thumb over the puckered skin. 'They're just scars. Marks of courage.'

Still holding her wrist, he moved her arm downward, tucking her against the strong wall of his body and bringing the goose-down covers up over her so that her back was against his chest, her arm cradled in his.

She sighed. 'That's one way of looking at it. To me they've always been marks of weakness. To my father, too. He can't bear to see it. I guess that's why I'm so self-conscious about it.'

Alejandro stiffened slightly. After a moment he said, 'Why? Why doesn't he like it?'

The curtains were open, and from where she lay Tamsin could see out into the moonwashed velvet sky. She felt like she was floating in space. The past seemed very distant, like she was looking at it through the wrong end of a telescope. Like it had happened to someone else.

'Well,' she said sleepily, 'because the accident was his fault, I guess.'

'What accident?'

Alejandro's mouth was close to her ear, his breath caressing her neck as he spoke. Tamsin stared out into an infinity of stars. Safe in his arms, she could speak without anguish.

'It was my birthday, my sixth birthday, and my father bought me a pony.'

Alejandro laughed shortly. 'Of course. What else?' he said in a voice that was tinged with mockery and a hint of an English upper-class accent.

'Well, one of those dolls with the hair you can style would have been my choice,' she said wryly. 'I was utterly terrified of horses.'

The fingers that were tracing delicate webs of pleasure over her hip slowed slightly. 'Why did he buy it, then?'

'He had no idea I was scared of them. To him, fear was weakness, so it was something I hid at all costs. Anyway, when this pony arrived, instead of being terribly grateful I refused to get on it.'

Her tone was rueful and ironic, but Alejandro could sense the pain that lurked deep beneath. He felt it in his own skin. Familiar hatred for Henry Calthorpe flared up, like an old wound opening.

'There was a terrible scene,' she went on quietly. 'He thought I was being rude and disobedient, and it became a matter of discipline that I had to do as I was told and get on the horse. In the end, he lifted me onto the bloody thing, and I was terrified so that I screamed and tried to get off straight away. I had my feet half out of the stirrups, and I was kicking, and he was shouting, and I guess it frightened the poor thing. It just took off. One of my feet was still caught in the stirrup, so I didn't fall off straight away.'

Holding her against him, Alejandro could feel the rapid beat of her heart beneath his forearm as the words spilled out of her in a breathless stream. Spikes of light burst behind his eyes as he pictured the scene she'd described. 'You were dragged?'

'No, not really,' she said with a half-hearted attempt at brightness. 'Well, not far, anyway.'

'You were bloody lucky it was only your arm that got broken.' His voice was like sandpaper.

'Oh, it wasn't. There were other things, but the elbow was the worst thing. The joint was completely shattered and I had to have lots of operations in the years that followed. That's why it's such a mess. And why it's not very strong.'

Tamsin's hair was soft against Alejandro's tense jaw. 'And what about your father? Did he apologise?'

'No.' It was a wistful sigh. 'He never mentioned it again. The pony must have been sent back while I was in hospital, and it was as if the whole thing never happened.'

Alejandro felt faint. 'God…'

'No; in a way it was the best thing he could have done. My mother and my sister would have wrapped me up in cotton wool—pink cotton-wool, probably—but he just carried on exactly as before. No sympathy, no allowances, no special treatment. It was good, really. I was so scared for a while, of being hurt again, but he made me hide it.'

Her words made him think of the time he'd challenged her to the game of pool. She'd played left-handed. No special treatment, she'd said. It seemed like a lifetime ago, when he'd thought she was spoiled and flaky.

'He made you hide the scars too, though.'

'Yes, that too.' Beneath the covers Alejandro felt her hand automatically go to her elbow, covering it in the way he'd seen her do so many times but hadn't understood. 'But he's right. They are hideous.'

He sat up suddenly, leaning over her in the dark. Against the pillow her face was as pale and cool as milk, her eyes shadowed and inexpressibly lovely. Alejandro spoke so fiercely it was little more than a growl. 'They're not hideous. I told you, they're a badge of honour. They show how strong you are.'

She raised her hand to his lips, the tips of her fingers lightly brushing the place where his lip had been split during the Barbarians game.

'You must have your share of them,' she said very softly.

He nodded. 'Hundreds.' For a long moment they just stared at each other. Alejandro felt his pulse begin to quicken, his tired, sore body harden again. She moved, raising herself up a little so that the sheet fell away, exposing her perfect breasts. She was astonishing. Ethereal in the gloom, she knelt up in front of him, pushing him down against the pillows and stroking her hand up his thigh.

'Let me see how many I can find…'

When Tamsin woke up she wasn't sure whether it was the misty violet light that was making everything look so absurdly beautiful, or the joy that glowed inside her newly awoken body.

Turning her head and looking up at Alejandro's sleeping face, she felt her heart blossom and burst, and knew it was the latter. A prison cell would look like paradise if she was waking up in it with him.

It was very early. Not yet morning, but no longer night. She wasn't sure how long they'd slept, tumbling into mutually sated oblivion with Alejandro's hand on her breast and his taste on her lips.

Her nipples hardened at the memory.

Beside her Alejandro stirred, pressing his lips to her bare shoulder, simultaneously caressing her tingling breast with one hand while sleepily lifting her arm with the other, and burying his mouth in the crook of her elbow. Tamsin felt a sensation like butterflies fluttering in the pit of her stomach, but she didn't pull away.

'The dress.' Behind her his voice was a growl, sexy and sleepy. 'That's why you didn't wear the dress I bought, isn't it?'

With a little wriggle of her hips, Tamsin flipped around so she was facing him, his sun tattoo level with her mouth. She kissed it.

'Good morning, sunshine,' she whispered with a smile, and then raised her head to look into his. Her insides melted with a mixture of raw desire and dreamy adoration. 'Yes. I'm sorry.'

'Where is it now?'

'In my room.'

In one fluid movement he got up and she watched him cross the room, too busy admiring his lean, brown back to wonder what he was doing. Grabbing a small towel from the *en-suite* bathroom, he slung it around his hips before pulling open the door and leaving the room.

He was back a moment later, the carrier bag in his hand.

Tamsin sat up, clutching the sheet to her chest and sweeping her hair back from her face. He stood at the foot of the bed, his eyes dark and hooded. Unshaven, he looked like a pirate. 'Come here.'

He took the dress out of the bag, letting it slip through his fingers like something living. Tamsin walked towards him, naked in the melting half-light, her head bowed, her eyes on his. He caught her hand, pulling her forward and positioning her in front of him as he stood in front of the big cheval glass.

For a second she was lost for words as she gazed at their reflection. He stood behind her, above her, his skin dark against hers, his powerful, muscular shoulders making her seem tiny by comparison. His hand held her waist, his fingers lightly spanning her ribs. They looked perfect together. Not just beautiful, but *right*.

And for the first time she could remember since the accident, her gaze didn't automatically go to her damaged arm.

His face was inscrutable as her eyes met his in the mirror. Slowly he picked up the dress, gathering it in his hands.

'Lift your arms.'

She did as she was told, like a person in a trance. The fabric felt luscious against her naked skin, and when she looked again she gave a little sighing gasp of surprise.

'Can you see how beautiful you are?' he said roughly.

'It's a beautiful dress,' she admitted.

'No. *You're* beautiful.' His fingers closed around her wrist, straightening her arm, exposing the scarred skin. 'Every inch of you. Can you see that?'

She looked. Maybe it wasn't so bad. He had looked at it and touched it and kissed it, after all. She smiled shyly, meeting his gaze in the mirror.

'I don't know. Perhaps.'

He turned away abruptly and went over to the damask-covered sofa at the foot of the huge bed. From the heap of clothes thrown down on it, he picked up a pair of polo breeches and pulled them on.

Tamsin felt a tiny dart of disappointment. 'Where are you going?'

He zipped up his boots and took her hand. 'You'll see,' he said curtly. 'You're coming with me.'

They stepped outside into a world of milky purity. The air was still cool, but with that damp, blue, hazy quality that holds the promise of heat later. Trailing across the glittering, dew-soaked grass, their fingers loosely entwined, neither of them spoke. With every step Tamsin's newly awakened body tingled and sang, and every time her shoulder brushed the bare skin of his arm tingles of bliss shimmered through her, like a meteor shower.

At the edge of the garden, where manicured formality gave way to untamed lushness, Alejandro let his fingers slide from hers.

'Wait here.'

He vaulted easily over the fence and walked away from her through the long grass of the field. He was wearing nothing but his polo breeches and knee-length boots, and she could see the muscles moving beneath the butterscotch skin of his back. Watching him melt into the blue mist, Tamsin felt weightless and dizzy with longing.

Everything was unreal, too perfect to be true. Leaning against the fence, she tipped her head back and closed her eyes, breathing in air that was as cool and clear as sparkling water. There was some small cynical voice in the darkest part of her heart that wanted to puncture this new-found bliss, and perversely she found herself thinking of Coronet, Sally, and the mountain of problems that awaited her in London. But in that moment, standing there in the opalescent dawn, she felt oddly at peace with it all.

As she heard the rumble of hoofbeats she opened her eyes and straightened up. Cantering towards her through the veils of mist on the pale-gold horse, Alejandro looked like some heroic prince from a story book, riding out into the world to seek his fortune or claim his bride. The frisson of familiar fear she felt as the horse came closer was dampened by the deafening beat of desire that instantly started up inside her as she looked up at him.

He slowed the horse to a walk, and it picked its way on delicate hooves through the long, wet grass. Sensing her uncertainty, Alejandro slid down from the saddle and came towards her.

'Alejandro…' Her tone hovered somewhere between an apology and a reproach.

'Shh.' He reached out and took her by the shoulders, stroking his thumb across her lips. 'There's nothing to be afraid of. I won't let anything bad happen. Here.' He drew her forward very gently. 'I wanted you to meet her.'

'I don't know, Alejandro.' But Tamsin knew that the frantic thud of her heart was nothing to do with being so close to the horse and everything to do with being close to Alejandro's broad, hard chest. The long grass was soaking the hem of her dress. His warm scent enveloped her, familiar and delicious as, taking her hand in his, he placed it on the horse's nose.

She jumped slightly as the horse lowered her head and blew down through her nostrils. Her nose felt like velvet, and her eyes were gentle, almost as gentle as Alejandro's fingers on her nape. As Tamsin ran her hand through the horse's silvery mane, Alejandro dropped his mouth to her shoulder, trailing a path of shivering kisses up the delicate skin of her neck, while his hand moulded one breast, teasing the nipple to hardness beneath the thin silk.

Clutching a handful of mane, Tamsin moaned.

'Do I take it you've got over your fear of horses?' he murmured into the side of her jaw.

'Mmm…I think it's what's called aversion therapy. You provide a distraction from the fear with—with another, stronger emotion.'

'In this case…?'

'In this case, the overwhelming desire to have sex with you in a field.'

He bent his head, and she watched the lines fan out at the corners of his eyes as he smiled a smile that sent another rush of liquid need pulsing down through her.

'Not here. We'll frighten the horses,' he said, putting his foot in the stirrup and swinging effortlessly up into the saddle.

'That would be a refreshing inversion of the norm,' Tamsin muttered, her hand instinctively going to her elbow as she took a step back. Left alone on the ground, her uncertainty returned.

'Come on.'

Alejandro was looking down at her, holding out his arms.

'No, I—' she protested, but he looked so strong, so solid, and so gorgeous, that she was lifting her arms even as she said it.

In a flurry of emerald silk he had lifted her up beside him, and his voice was low and warm in her ear. 'Good girl. I've got you. You're safe.'

His arm was tight around her waist. The movement of the horse beneath her was an undulating sway, and Tamsin gave a gasp of surprise and delight. 'Oh, Alejandro, it's amazing! I'm doing it—I'm riding!'

'If you take to this as naturally as you've taken to your other new-found skill, I'd better sign you up for the San Silvana team,' he murmured, and desire rippled through Tamsin's body like the wind through her hair. The pressure of the saddle against her bare flesh was a reminder of past ecstasy and a promise of pleasure to come. She swung her legs and felt her hips undulating in time to the movement of the horse.

'Faster.'

It was a low, breathless plea.

Alejandro pulled her closer to him. She could feel the pressure of his arousal against the small of her back, and the hard muscles of his thighs flexing as he urged the horse forward into a languid canter.

Tamsin gave a high cry of pleasure.

It was like flying.

The sun was just beginning to come up, leaving only a veil of mist lying low over the grass, so it felt like riding over the clouds. The fluid silk of her dress billowed up around her bare legs and her hair blew back from her face. Ahead of them San Silvana languished in the golden morning light like an enchanted palace.

The horse's hooves clattered on the gravel as Alejandro gently eased its pace, bringing her to a halt in front of the steps. Dropping the reins, letting go of Tamsin's waist, he placed his hands on her knees and brought them slowly up her thighs beneath the silk dress. Tamsin lifted her arms above her head, anchoring them around his strong neck as she arched her back and tilted her hips forward.

The horse shifted beneath them, and Alejandro's thumbs met the slippery wetness at the top of Tamsin's legs.

His low moan of longing was muffled in her hair, and then he jumped lightly down and held up his arms to her. The expression of blazing lust on his face turned her insides to water.

'You have precisely fifteen seconds before I combust with desire,' she said softly as he took her into his arms. 'Do you think we can make it upstairs in time?'

CHAPTER FIFTEEN

'THAT was completely delicious.'

With a sigh of total contentment, Tamsin collapsed back against the pillows. Alejandro laughed softly, removing the tray of croissants and coffee and placing it on the table beside the bed.

'Are you referring to breakfast, or what came directly before it?'

'Well, I was thinking about breakfast, actually, but now you come to mention it the starter was particularly lovely too.' Closing her eyes, she slid one bare foot up his leg and ran her tongue lasciviously over her lips. 'I think, Mr D'Arienzo, I may have to have you tested for performance enhancing drugs. But first I may just have to test your performance one more time...'

Alejandro felt the blood rush into his groin again, and it took all of his considerable self-control to kiss her lightly on one peachy shoulder and get out of bed.

'Not now. There's some business I have to see to.' He crossed the room to the huge, old mahogany chest of drawers and began pulling out clothes. If he didn't get dressed and get out of the room soon, the sight of her naked body in the tangle of sheets would prove too much, and the rest of the day would be lost in sensual oblivion.

The thought of which was tempting. In fact, irresistible, but he had to make these calls. For her sake.

'Get some sleep,' he said huskily as he opened the door and looked back at her. With her white-blonde hair tousled and her lips reddened and swollen from his kisses, she looked sweet and wanton and gorgeous. 'You'll need it for what I've got planned for you later.'

Her eyes widened and her mouth curved into a smile of pure wicked invitation, and he had to force himself to leave. As he strode along the corridor, desire zig-zagged through him like forked lightning, and he hoped this share buy-up was going to be straightforward. Then tonight they could celebrate Coronet's salvation in style.

In bed.

Tamsin's first thought when she woke up was that she'd dreamed it all. It had happened so many times: her night of deep and secret passion in the arms of Alejandro D'Arienzo, shattered by the shrill of the bell, and she would open her eyes and find herself back in the freezing dorm at school on another grey morning.

Fat slabs of buttery sunlight fell across the bed, and the green-silk dress and Alejandro's polo breeches lay abandoned on the floor. Stretching out between the rumpled sheets, she breathed in the musky scent of their love-making, and was pierced through with a shaft of pleasure so pure it made her gasp.

Not a dream. Real. But almost too perfect to be believed.

Looking at her watch, Tamsin was amazed to find that it was early afternoon. She scrambled out of bed and grabbed a towel from the bathroom to wrap around herself while she went back to her own room.

Everything was as she'd left it last night when she'd changed for the party and her heart had been as heavy as lead. As she moved around the room, picking up clothes and tidying away make-up, happiness bubbled up inside her. So much had changed since then; it felt like thick, heavy curtains had been drawn back and her life lay in front of her, glittering with promise.

Absently she picked up her mobile, lying as it was amid the chaos on the dressing table, and checked the calls. Serena had tried to ring, several times, and her father too. Her heart gave a tiny lurch of apprehension as she imagined how he'd react if he knew how she'd spent the last twelve hours. In time she'd tell him, but right now she just wanted to talk to someone who would share her joy.

But just as she was about to dial Serena the phone came to life in her hands, ringing and vibrating simultaneously, and making her jump out of her skin. Laughing, she held it to her ear, making a serious effort to control her amusement as she heard the dry, precise voice of Jim Atkinson, her accountant.

'Tamsin, we have a problem,' he said without preamble.

Tamsin felt the smile die on her lips. Twisting the silver ring around her thumb, she felt a cold sensation creep up from her stomach.

'What's the matter, Jim?'

'We're not entirely sure.' He gave a nervous laugh. 'It's all highly unusual—unprecedented, in fact—for such dramatic activity to take place over such a short period of time. We're still trying to make sense of how this could have happened, but I felt I had to let you know as soon as possible.'

Somewhere in the back of Tamsin's mind an alarm bell was ringing. She gave her head an abrupt shake. 'Sorry, Jim, let me know *what,* exactly?'

'There's been a lot of activity involving the company's shares on the stock market today. All of the shares available on the open market were sold at the start of trading this morning.'

Tamsin's grip on the phone relaxed a little. 'Well, that's OK, isn't it? I mean, there can't have been that many shares available, so even if they've been bought by one individual it's not a major threat to the company. The majority are owned by me and Sally.'

There was a pause, and seven-thousand miles away in London Jim Atkinson cleared his throat. 'It appears that that may no longer be the case,' he said in a subdued voice. 'About two hours ago another large number of shares were sold, which as far as we can tell could only have come from one of you. I'm assuming you haven't released any yourself?'

'No.' Tamsin's voice was hoarse. 'But Sally wouldn't…'

The words petered out. 'Well,' Jim said gravely, 'as I said, it's most irregular. We're still trying to make sense of the limited information available, but I'm afraid it appears that we're looking at a hostile-takeover bid.'

'But who would do that? And *why*?' she moaned.

'I just don't know. I'll get back to you the minute I can tell you anything.' He paused, and Tamsin waited for him to tell her not to worry, as he had done so many times in the past, that it was a simple enough matter to sort out.

'Tamsin, I'm sorry,' he said quietly.

For a moment after the line went dead she held the phone in her hand, staring down at it as her head swam sickeningly. In the sunny, serene room it was almost possible to believe she'd just imagined that whole conversation.

Almost possible and, oh, so tempting.

Outside, the day that had started so magically was now heavy and golden. Her body still throbbed with repletion, and downstairs in his office Alejandro was working, maybe even distracted by the same memories of last night that flickered tantalisingly through her head. Jim was overreacting, she thought with a surge of optimism. He was obsessively cautious—that was what made him so good at his job, after all. He'd phone in a little while and tell her it was all sorted and there was nothing to worry about.

She gave a little cry as, right on cue, the phone in her hand began to ring.

'Jim!'

'Darling, you've obviously been away too long.' The familiar voice was clipped and sardonic. 'You've forgotten your own father. Hardly surprising, since you haven't called home in almost a week.'

'Sorry, Daddy. I was expecting a call from Jim Atkinson.'

'Oh? Problems?'

'I don't know. Something about a lot of shares being bought very quickly. He was muttering about hostile takeovers, but he's probably over-dramatising. I can't think why anyone would want to take over Coronet. Anyway, other than that, everything's fine. Apart from sponsors, the Pumas strip is well underway, and Alejandro has asked me to stay on and design shirts for his polo team.'

She felt herself blushing as she said his name, and was glad that Henry couldn't see. Nervousness was making her talk too much, and she had to stop before she found herself blurting out more than would be wise at this stage. But she needn't have worried. There was a long silence on the other end of the phone, and when Henry spoke again his voice was stiff and distant, almost as if he hadn't been listening.

'Does Atkinson know who's bought the shares?'

'No, not at the moment. He thinks that Sally might have sold hers, but that's impossible. She'd never do anything like that without telling me first.'

'Unless someone told her to keep it from you until it was too late.'

Tamsin gave an uncertain laugh. 'You sound like Jim. Who would do that?'

Henry sighed heavily. 'Someone who knows you're out of the country. Someone who wants to hurt you.'

Tamsin's heartbeat quickened painfully as anger warmed her blood. 'Oh, I see where this is going,' she said quietly. 'You're trying to say it's Alejandro. You just can't get past the fact that you *don't like* him, can you, Daddy? You think that just because he didn't fit in with the rest of your respectable English public-school boys—'

'No.' Henry's voice was heavy with regret as he cut her off. 'It's not that. It's because he has good reason to want to hurt you, Tamsin. Look, I really didn't want to have to say all this, but I suppose I should have talked to you before you left.' He hesitated, then said bleakly, 'About the circumstances under which he left.'

'What do you mean?'

'It was because of what happened that night at Harcourt. Because of you.'

The room seemed to sway slightly. The sunlight coming through the tall windows was suddenly hard and dazzling. Tamsin put a hand up to her head. 'What do you mean?' she said faintly. 'You said you didn't trust him.'

'With you. I didn't trust him with *you*.' Henry spoke as if he were in pain. 'I knew how infatuated with him you were—all those pictures in your room, the sudden interest in rugby. I knew he'd only hurt you, and then that night at Harcourt when I caught him coming out of the orangery I—'

'You sacked him because of that?'

'Yes.'

Tamsin's voice was a cracked whisper. 'That's so *unfair*!'

'Tamsin, I'm sorry. I was trying to protect you. I handled it badly, I know that now.'

Mindlessly Tamsin rubbed her elbow as her mind staggered to get a hold of reality. 'So, you think he's doing this to back at me?' she murmured through bloodless lips. 'He lost his job because of me, and now he's trying to take my company from me?'

'I could be wrong.' Henry's tone was brisk now. 'It might not be him. I'm just warning you…'

Letting the phone drop to her side, Tamsin very quietly cut the call while he was still speaking and sank down onto the bed. She felt sick. There was a sharp, stabbing pain somewhere inside her, radiating out from her chest. For a long time she just sat numbly, waiting for something, without quite knowing what it was.

And then the phone rang again, and Jim Atkinson's voice spoke to her from half a world away, and the pain intensified into a searing blaze of agonising fury.

'I've discovered the name of the buyer for Sally's shares,' he said soberly. 'It's a company based in Buenos Aires. They're called San Silvana Holdings.'

'I need to speak to Alejandro.'

Giselle was out of her seat in a flash, placing herself in front of the door to Alejandro's office and crossing her arms. She reminded Tamsin of some sleek, pedigree cat; in spite of the casual pose, Tamsin just knew that if she had a tail she would be lashing it now.

'I'm afraid he's busy,' she purred. 'But I'll tell him that you wished to see him.'

'It's urgent.'

Giselle shrugged elegantly. 'Sorry.' Malice glinted in her eyes. 'It's very important business, and he specifically asked that you should not be admitted.'

Of course, thought Tamsin in horror. *She's in on all this. I knew from the start that she hated me, and now I know why. She's been involved all along.*

Adrenalin burned through her veins like acid. She was shaking with fury, and hurt. 'How thorough of him. Maybe he didn't realise that I'd find out exactly what kind of "very important business" it is through my own channels.' She raised her head and met Giselle's hostile gaze. 'I was prepared to do him the courtesy of giving him the chance to explain, but I'm afraid I'm not going to wait around while he finishes taking everything I have. Tell him I said goodbye.'

'Certainly.' She had just reached the door when Giselle added in the same cool, superior tone, 'Is there anything else I can help with?'

Tamsin hesitated. 'Yes. You can arrange a car to take me to the airport. I'm sure that'll give you great satisfaction.'

By the time Alejandro put the phone down his head ached and his shoulders were rigid with tension. He dragged a hand over his unshaven jaw and leaned back in his chair.

What a day.

It was just past five. He hadn't stopped since he'd left Tamsin after breakfast this morning, and he suddenly realised how hungry he was. Hungry and tired, meaning that dinner in the same place where they'd shared breakfast would be good. Preferably with the same hors d'oeuvres, and plenty of champagne to toast Coronet's new beginning without its second director.

The answer had been lurking at the back of his mind all the time, but it had all fallen into place this morning when he'd looked back over the file of cuttings and company information he'd compiled the other night. A single phone call to Sally at the Coronet office, pretending to be a buyer from Dubai interested in placing some fake Coronet designs in his shop, had yielded instant results.

Sally could hardly have denied any of the accusations he'd levelled at her after that. Neither had she been in any position to refuse to hand over her shares, all of which were now registered safely under the name of a couple of his companies, awaiting transfer back to Tamsin.

Tamsin…

He stretched, his mind drifting back to this morning—riding through the dawn mist with her in front of him, the feel of her hot, wet body as he'd pulled her down into his arms, the excitement that had shone from her lovely eyes.

Instantly he was as hard as hell. Closing down his computer, he got up, suddenly impatient to see her for reasons that had nothing whatsoever to do with shares.

By the time Tamsin had arrived at Ezeiza airport the last remaining flight to London was fully booked. Unable to bear the thought of waiting in the airport overnight, she had simply enquired which flights did have seats available, and had booked herself onto the next plane to Barcelona.

Numbness had descended on her like some inbuilt opiate as she eased herself into the cramped seat, dulling the terrible pain in her heart until it was a generalised ache that spread through her whole body.

The plane seemed to wait an eternity to take off. Around her, other passengers were getting restless, and the stewardesses fluttered between them, smoothing frayed nerves and shooting each other uncertain glances. Eventually there was a commotion at the door, and everyone tensed as a uniformed man appeared at the front of the plane with one of the stewardesses.

He was looking in Tamsin's direction, and suddenly she recognised him as the customs official who had searched her on Alejandro's plane.

'Lady Calthorpe. Come with me, please.'

Leaden with shock, Tamsin did as she was told, oblivious to the curious glances of the other passengers as she climbed clumsily over the long legs of the backpacker next to her. Her heart was thudding so hard it felt like it might break out of her chest, but it missed a beat as she came to the front of the plane and saw Alejandro standing in the small space at the top of the steps.

His massive shoulders filled the doorway, blocking out the light beyond, his back towards her. Her throat constricted around a twisted knot of emotion, and tears prickled her eyes. She put her hand up to her mouth as he turned round. The expression on his face was chilling.

'Don't tell me, you suddenly had an overwhelming urge to see the sights of Barcelona?' His voice as always was perfectly controlled, but it was as taut as razor wire.

Tamsin lifted her chin, leaning against the wall of the cabin and trying to stop herself from shaking.

'Hardly,' she said with stinging bitterness. 'I had a sudden overwhelming urge to get home and try to salvage what's left of my business.' She gave a short, scathing laugh, gesturing around the cramped interior of the plane. 'Of course, I should have known that it wouldn't be that simple. Corruption is second nature to you, isn't it, Alejandro? Bribing customs officials and holding up a plane is nothing to a man who's prepared to *sleep* with someone while he's planning to strip them of everything they own.'

The noise level in the cabin behind her was rising as the other passengers were getting increasingly impatient, but Tamsin was aware only of Alejandro. His eyes had darkened from gold to dull bronze, and a muscle was flickering in his stubble-darkened jaw. His face bore the same expression of dangerous calm she had seen on the polo field.

'Don't judge people by your own standards, Tamsin,' he said very quietly. 'I'm trying to *help* you.'

A stewardess appeared, looking extremely agitated. 'If I could ask you to hurry, please…' she began sharply, then, seeing the expression on Alejandro's dark, beautiful face, backed off.

'Trying to help?' Tamsin hissed. 'What, by staging a hostile takeover of my company? I've got to hand it to you, my accountant had never seen anything like it. We didn't stand a chance, but then I suppose that's hardly surprising. You're as ruthless as you are cold and unscrupulous.'

'I'm touched that you think so highly of me,' he said with biting sarcasm. 'I should have realised you only accept help when it's offered in such a way as to make it appear you've done the work yourself. My mistake.'

Tamsin gasped. 'What are you talking about?'

'The RFU commission; what was it you said, you got it on merit? You had to compete?' Alejandro laughed softly. 'I don't think so. Yours was the only proposal that was passed to the board.'

She felt like she'd swallowed a hot coal. Vehemently she shook her head. 'No! That's not true…'

The captain appeared, laying an apologetic hand on Alejandro's shoulder. 'Alejandro, my friend, please.' He made a helpless gesture to the body of the plane, in which the atmosphere was growing more restless.

Alejandro nodded tersely, his eyes burning into Tamsin's. For a long moment they looked at each other. Tamsin felt like she was falling, falling, and that somewhere there was a cord that would open a parachute, but she didn't know how to find it. Alejandro's face was ashen, with lines of fatigue etched around eyes that blazed with emotion. And then, with a look that was almost like despair, he turned and walked down the steps.

Tamsin's breath caught in her throat as iron bands gripped her chest. She wanted to speak, to cry out and make him turn round, but she was suffocating, gasping, and then the gentle hands of the stewardess took her shoulders and guided her back into the cabin, towards her seat.

A grim cheer of satisfaction went up from the passengers as, seven minutes late, the plane left the runway and surged upwards. But as it climbed higher and higher into the faded blue evening the falling sensation Tamsin had felt earlier intensified. It was peaceful and unreal, but she closed her eyes tightly and waited helplessly for the agonising moment when she hit the ground.

CHAPTER SIXTEEN

Four months later.

TWICKENHAM on match day always had a carnival atmosphere, and today, with the crowds basking in unexpectedly warm spring sunshine, the mood was particularly celebratory. The Six Nations tournament had finished, and in the stands there was a laid back, end-of-term sense of excitement about the prospect of a friendly match. Los Pumas were formidable opponents, and the game promised to be hugely entertaining.

In the luxurious comfort of the members' lounge, Tamsin felt cut off from the good-humoured crowd in every way possible.

Beside her Serena leaned back in her chair and rested her empty plate on the huge mountain of her stomach. 'I wonder if the team medics have experience of delivering babies,' she said dreamily. Tamsin glanced at her in alarm.

'You don't think that you might… What, now? Here?'

'No, I shouldn't think so,' Serena sighed. 'I don't actually think this baby's ever going to be born. I'm just going to go on getting fatter and fatter until I can't move at all. Talking of which, would you mind awfully getting me another of those lovely anchovy things?'

Tamsin stood up quickly and took the plate from Serena's bump, glad of the excuse to do something, however trivial. She felt restless to the point of panic. The long room with its balcony over the pitch was filled with rugby dignitaries from both England and Argentina, making the most of the lavish hospitality. Tamsin was haunted by the thought that the tanned, elegant Pumas contingent must all be colleagues of Alejandro's, and found herself desperately eavesdropping on their conversations in the hope of hearing his name.

She was that pitiful.

'Just the anchovy thing, or would you like some kiwi fruit and mayonnaise with that?' she asked with a wan smile. 'In fact, you don't even have to answer. I like to think I'm something of an expert on your insane cravings now. Leave it to me.'

'You can laugh,' Serena called after her. 'But you just wait! One day it'll be your bottom that's the size of Denmark, and your fridge that's full of mayonnaise, and my teasing will be merciless.'

Reaching across the table where the buffet was laid out, Tamsin felt her smile die as knives of anguish sliced into her. It was utterly inconceivable that the air of voluptuous, milky contentment that cocooned Serena in the final weeks of her pregnancy would ever be hers. Barren survival was about as much as she could hope for, and that was in her more positive moments. She had smashed her own fragile chance of happiness when she had so brutally misjudged the man who'd held it in his hands.

'Tamsin.'

She jumped, jerking the plate upwards and sending anchovies and kiwi fruit flying. 'Please, darling,' Henry Calthorpe said gently. 'Don't run away. I just wanted to say how glad I am that you came today. How proud I am of you.'

Tamsin ducked her head and struggled to pick up a slice of kiwi fruit between shaking fingers. It kept sliding out of her grasp. 'At least the Pumas commission is one that I really did get on my own merit,' she muttered bitterly.

'*Touché*,' Henry said dryly, sliding more fruit onto Serena's plate. 'I deserve that.' He hesitated for a moment before continuing in an awkward undertone. 'Look, darling, I know this is hardly the time or the place, but I've been wanting to talk to you since the day you got home. I know you were angry then and you wouldn't listen, but I just want to say I'm sorry. I've handled everything so badly; I know that. Your mother always says that I have to let you go and watch you fall. But…' He faltered. 'I did that once and I've never been able to forgive myself.'

Tamsin sighed and shook her head sadly as she put the plate down. 'It all comes back to the accident, doesn't it?'

Henry nodded. 'I was responsible, and I felt so guilty. But it also brought home to me how fragile you are underneath that tough exterior, and how much I love you. I knew it was important not to wrap you up in cotton wool after that, but I couldn't bear to watch you struggle. I just wanted you to be safe.'

'You can't rearrange the world like that, Daddy.'

'Why not?' A look of anger passed across Henry's patrician face. 'It's a natural instinct. I can't bear the thought of anyone hurting you.'

'Yes, well, *you* hurt me,' Tamsin said in a low voice. 'You diminished me. You made it clear that you think I'm not capable of achieving things myself, or…or being loved for who I am, scars and all.'

Her throat burned with the effort of holding in the huge sob that was building inside her. Every word took her back to Alejandro, and lying curled up against him as the day broke, letting him touch and kiss the shameful, damaged part of her.

It took her breath away to think now about how monstrously she'd misjudged him. He'd been so tender, so perfect, and in the space of one magical night had taught her so much.

So much.

But even so, when faced with uncertainty she had instantly assumed the worst about him. She'd realised exactly how wrong she'd been when she'd arrived back in England and found all the shares in her name, and Sally gone. Alejandro had seen what had been right in front of her all the time; had seen it and dealt with it. It was Sally who had betrayed her.

Not him.

'So, will you accept my apology?' prompted Henry gently. Around them the excitement was mounting, and a blast of spring air hit them as the doors onto the balcony opened and people went outside. Tamsin looked up at Henry and gave a swift, painful smile. 'It's not your fault,' she admitted. 'Not entirely, anyway, though you have to promise me that you won't—'

She broke off as Serena appeared beside them—or, rather, the huge mound of Serena's stomach appeared, with Serena some distance behind. 'I'm fading away from hunger over there,' she grumbled before stopping abruptly. 'Oh, God, sorry, I'm interrupting something important, aren't I?'

Tamsin shook her head. 'No, it's fine. I was just warning Dad that if he ever interferes in my life again I shall change my name and move to the other side of the world.'

Henry and Serena exchanged a meaningful look.

'OK, well the game will be starting soon,' said Serena in an oddly bright voice, hustling Tamsin towards the door. 'I really think we should go and find Simon. He'll be in the company box knocking back corporate champagne, but I don't want him to miss the moment when your brilliant shirts first appear, Tam. Are you excited about seeing them?'

Letting Serena drag her out into the corridor, Tamsin felt her stomach lurch.

The shirts she'd never seen and had had no control over, since Alejandro hadn't returned her phone calls. The shirts she'd designed with his body in mind. The shirts that in a few short minutes were going to be mocking her fifteen times over with memories that burned into her head like acid.

'Excited' was hardly the word. She felt like a driver looking into the twisted wreckage of the car that had nearly killed her.

Fascinated, maybe. But not in a good way.

Alejandro tipped his head back and closed his eyes, listening to the roaring chant of the crowd echoing around the stadium, counting the passing seconds by the painful thud of his heart.

The last few moments before the start of a game were always the worst, but never before had he felt tension like this. Sitting alone in semi-darkness in a VIP-hospitality-box, he almost wished he was down there in the dressing room preparing to go out onto the pitch, but at the same time he recognised that the competitive buzz that had always driven him was suddenly utterly absent. In a few moments Argentina would be taking on England out there, and Alejandro couldn't care less who won.

It was a game. Nothing more.

In his hands he held a single sheet of thick, pale-blue notepaper, covered on both sides in spiky black handwriting. Henry Calthorpe's letter had reached him via the offices of the Argentine Rugby Union, and he had received it when he'd arrived for the board meeting where the sponsors for the new kit were to be decided.

It had rocked him to the core, which accounted for the rather rash offer he now felt so uncertain about.

He expelled a long, shaky breath and dropped his head into his hands. What the hell had Tamsin Calthorpe done to him? Control had always been paramount to him. Control and focus and drive, and yet she had turned him into a man who held up aeroplanes, who could focus on nothing but the remembered feel of her skin against his, and the scent of her hair, who caused a stir in board meetings by making hugely inflated, last-minute sponsorship offers.

He shook his head helplessly as he remembered the look of astonishment on the faces of the board members around the table as he'd made his offer. It was one way of livening up a board meeting, he thought acidly. And every one of those present had found room in their diaries to make the trip to Twickenham for this game.

Abruptly he got up and went to stand at the window, his whole body rigid. In his career Alejandro had coped with agony and injury. He was used to physical pain. He could deal with it, understand it, work around it.

But this mental agony was different. It tortured him, so that in his blacker moments he knew that he would do anything to be free of it.

Kill or cure.

That was why he was here. That was why he was about to lay his pride and his reputation bare before a watching world. Because if Tamsin didn't want him, if she didn't come, he was ruined anyway.

'It must be pregnancy hormones,' moaned Serena, slowing down and leaning against the wall of the plush corridor inside the west stand for a moment. 'I can't remember where he said the box was. Have you tried that door there?'

'There's no name on the door, so it's probably not in use,' said Tamsin patiently. 'Look, don't worry; he's probably back in the members' lounge by now. Let's go back and—'

'No! Just try the door, please, Tamsin.'

Even in the insulated comfort of the VIP corridor they were both aware that the atmosphere in the ground had changed. The noise of the shouting and singing had cranked up a level, and from far below they could hear the sound of a band playing.

'Please, Tam,' said Serena, and there was a note of desperation in her voice that made it impossible not to obey. 'Hurry. We're going to miss the start.'

'OK.' Exasperated, Tamsin opened the door. Instantly the noise from the stadium reached them more loudly, but the room itself was quiet and unlit. She took a step forward. 'See, there's no-one here—'

She gasped and her heart leapt into her throat as she caught sight of the figure silhouetted against the glass wall of the box. For a moment those broad, powerful shoulders, the narrow hips, had reminded her of...

'No one? I was hoping you'd stopped seeing me in those terms.'

The familiar low, ironic drawl sent tidal waves of emotion smashing through her. In an instant her frozen body was brought back to life. She could feel the colour flood into her cheeks, the heat surge through her pelvis, just at the sound of his voice.

And then he came towards her in the dim light, and she saw him properly.

The world stopped.

His remote, warrior face was pale, the shadows around his eyes almost as dark as the bruise he'd had when she'd seen him at Twickenham that last time. For a moment she could do nothing but gaze at him, unable to take in that he was really there. Then, aware that she was staring, she dropped her head, a blush of confusion and shame deepening in her cheeks.

'Sorry. I thought—I meant—I didn't think there was anyone in here.' She gave a nervous start as behind her the heavy door swung shut with a muffled bang. 'I didn't think *you* were here at all,' she whispered. 'I'm sorry. I wouldn't have come if I'd known.'

She made to turn round again and open the door, but he held his arm across it to bar her way. Tamsin took an abrupt step back to avoid touching him.

'Which would have meant I'd travelled seven-thousand miles for nothing.'

His voice was like gravel. Tamsin couldn't bear to look up into his face.

'You've come to see the game,' she muttered, looking distractedly out at the huge expanse of sunlit pitch beyond the glass. It seemed unreal.

'No. I've come to see you.'

She gave a short laugh, which seemed to hitch in her throat. 'You could have just phoned me back.'

Both of them were being very careful to stand a little distance apart from each other, but now he reached out and took her shoulders in his hands, looking down into her face. He was frowning. 'Phoned you back—you rang me?'

Tamsin nodded. 'I left a message with Giselle.'

Rolling his eyes, he let her go, and thrust his hands into his pockets. 'That must have been a while ago. I sacked her a few days after you left.' He walked over to the huge wall of glass that looked out over the pitch. 'What was the message?'

Tamsin stayed where she was, by the door.

'Sorry,' she said quietly. 'Sorry for being so quick to jump to conclusions. Sorry for not trusting you.'

'Obviously all that was too complicated for Giselle to grasp,' he said with heavy sarcasm. 'Was there anything else?'

Behind him the pre-match display was coming to an end, but it was as if the electric atmosphere out there in the massive arena had been captured and crammed into the small space where they stood facing each other.

'Yes,' Tamsin said, and took a few hesitant steps towards him. 'I told her to say thank you for what you did for Coronet. I was so stupid, not guessing what Sally was doing, and without you I would have lost everything—' She faltered, absently rubbing her elbow as the irony of those words hit her.

She *was* without him, and she had lost everything.

'Was that all?'

'Yes,' she said dully, keeping her eyes fixed to the floor. There was a long pause. 'No,' she added in a whisper. 'There was more, but… Oh, it doesn't matter…'

She made the mistake of looking up then. His face was shuttered and barred, a mask of indifference, but his eyes burned into hers with an intensity that made her heart falter.

'What?' he said mockingly. 'That you're madly in love with me and you can't live without me?'

Pain tore through her with the ferocity of a blow torch. 'Don't laugh! That's exactly what it was. But don't worry; I know it's completely unreasonable, and that's why I didn't say it! I know how badly I've treated you, how much suffering I've brought to you—'

'I don't think you do,' he moaned, thrusting his hand through his hair. As he pushed it back from his forehead, Tamsin could see the lines of anguish there.

'I'm sorry,' she said hopelessly as a fat tear slid down her cheek, closely followed by another. 'What I did was unforgivable; I know that. It's my fault. I blew it, and now too much has happened and there are too many things between us for it to be possible that we could ever be…'

Her voice cracked. Through a haze of tears she was aware of the tormented tenderness on his face as he took her hand and pulled her to him, opening the door onto the private balcony of the box.

'Oh dear.' He spoke so softly his voice was barely audible above the noise of the crowd. 'In that case I'm about to be humiliated very, very publicly…'

Out on the field the teams were coming out. Very gently he drew her forward to the railing at the front of the balcony, keeping his eyes fixed on her face as the Pumas players filed out.

Tamsin gave a whimper of disbelief, and the crowd erupted into a tumult of screaming and applause. One by one the players turned so they were facing the box where she stood in front of Alejandro, his hands resting on her waist.

In the place she had intended the sponsor's name to appear each shirt bore a different word. As the fifteenth player, whose shirt showed only a question mark, joined the line, the sentence was complete:

TAMSIN CALTHORPE I LOVE YOU SO VERY MUCH PLEASE PLEASE WILL YOU MARRY ME?

The players stood, impassive, heroic, blazing their message of love while the spellbound crowd stilled expectantly. Tamsin turned round to face him, her eyes wide and shining with tears, her mouth opening wordlessly as she struggled to take it in.

He caught her face between his hands. 'You have no idea how much it stretched my creative powers to convey that message in exactly fifteen words,' he moaned softly against her cheek, before finding her lips with his in a kiss that was filled with desperate, hopeful tenderness.

A minute later he pulled gently away, and looked at her with eyes that were opaque with anguish and love.

'I really hate to break this off, because I have wanted to kiss the living daylights out of you every minute of every day for the past four months—but do you realise that I, and eighty-thousand other people, am waiting for your answer?'

'Yes,' she breathed. 'My answer is yes. Now, will you please kiss me again?'

And he did. Pulling her roughly against him, he cupped the back of her head with one hand, and the thumbs-up sign he did with the other was picked up by the zoom lens of the cameraman below and beamed onto the big screens.

As a roar of delight went round the crowd, the Pumas players leapt up, punching the air and embracing each other in celebration. On the balcony of the members' lounge some distance away more champagne was opened, spraying the crowd below with plumes of foam as grinning Argentine officials shook hands with tearful Calthorpes.

Without letting his mouth leave hers, Alejandro scooped Tamsin up and carried her back inside, closing the door as the band started playing.

'It's completely disrespectful,' he murmured hoarsely, setting her down and sliding his hands underneath her top as they both sank to the floor. 'But I'm sure that just this once it won't matter if we don't stand up for the national anthems…'

EPILOGUE

A DRIFT of confetti fluttered from Tamsin's hair as Alejandro dropped her onto the bed in the jet's small cabin. He kicked the door shut, and then turned back to her with a smile that made her wriggle with ecstatic anticipation.

'Did I tell you how beautiful you look today?' he said huskily, dropping a kiss onto her collarbone as she rose up onto her knees and wrapped her arms around his neck.

'Only about a hundred times.' She smiled. 'But it's a long flight. You have time to mention it quite a bit more before we get to San Silvana.'

Alejandro reached over and lifted a bottle of champagne out of the ice box where Alberto had left it for them. Tamsin felt weak with longing as she watched his strong, practised fingers tear the foil off. 'Sorry,' he said nonchalantly, handing her a glass of golden bubbles. 'I intend to get that delicious slip of a dress off you in the next couple of minutes, and then conversation isn't really on my agenda for the next fifteen hours. So I'll say it one more time.' He bent to kiss her lingeringly, his warm hand moving over her back to the zip of the dress as he murmured gravely against her mouth, 'Tamsin D'Arienzo, you are the most incredibly, unreasonably, excruciatingly lovely bride ever.'

In one lithe movement Tamsin stood up and let the dress fall to the floor in a papery rustle of silk. Alejandro gave a moan of naked longing as she stood before him in her ivory silk stockings and the briefest, sheerest pair of silk pants with 'just married' embroidered across them.

'Come here,' he said thickly.

Tamsin was a mass of quivering, wanton longing in his arms by the time he finally dragged his mouth from hers and leaned over to open the drawer of the bedside cabinet.

She gave a gasp of realisation as he rummaged with increasing exasperation through the contents of the drawer. Pulling him back down onto the bed, she bit her lip to suppress the wicked, delicious smile that was building inside her.

'Darling,' she breathed, taking his face in her hands and brushing her lips against his cheek. 'What would you say to the idea of a honeymoon baby…?'

 **MILLS & BOON®**

and

ENGLAND RUGBY

present

INTERNATIONAL BILLIONAIRES

*From rich tycoons to royal playboys –
they're red-hot and ruthless*

Read all about the players, the glamour,
the excitement of the game – and where to
escape when you want some romance!

A GIRL'S GUIDE TO RUGBY

Rugby isn't just thirty sweaty men getting muddy in a field for eighty minutes – although that can be quite appealing! It's played in more than a hundred countries across five continents, by all ages and sexes. It's a fun, fast and furious spectator sport – and it's also a great family day out.

International locations
Want some winter sun? Jet off to **Dubai** for the International Rugby Sevens. Or pop to **Argentina** for a spot of tango, polo *and* rugby. Or how about a trip to **Sydney** for the **Tri Nations**?

Glamorous audience
Don't forget to keep an eye out for celebrities watching the game with you! You might spot **Prince William** and **Prince Harry** at Twickenham, or **Charlotte Church** cheering for Gavin Henson at the Millennium Stadium in Cardiff. **Zara Phillips** is also dating a rugby player.

Not just for the boys
Who knows? You may be inspired to have a go yourself! Rugby is one of the best all-round **workouts**, building strength, cardiovascular fitness and toning those all-important wobbly bits. And nothing is better than being part of a winning team!

ENGLAND
RUGBY

Rugby — the basics

First time at a match? Always wondered what a line-out was? Confused by an offside call? These basic facts will get you through!

1. **Vital statistics**
   There are fifteen players on each side. Each match lasts for eighty minutes, and the team plays forty minutes in one direction and then they swap ends.

2. **Scoring**
   The object is to score more points than the opposition. Teams can score a try, penalty, drop goal or conversion.

3. **Try**
   When the ball is grounded over the try line and within the area before the dead ball line it earns five points.

4. **Conversion**
   After a team scores a try, a conversion, a free kick at goal from a point directly in line with where the try was scored, is worth two points.

5. **Drop goal**
   When, in open play, the ball is kicked between the rugby post uprights and above the crossbar, in a drop goal, it earns three points.

6. **Penalty**
   This can be awarded by the referee for infringements of the rules of rugby and if successfully kicked it earns three points.

7. **Offside**
   This is the key rule of rugby, and it's a lot simpler than football. Say your friend has the ball and she passes it to you. If she has to throw

it *back* to you, you are onside. If she throws it *forward*, you are offside. Players must be behind the ball.

8. **Tackle**
   Not as rude as it sounds! The player with the ball is brought to the ground by a tackle, and they must either pass or release the ball.

9. **Ruck**
   If a player loses possession of the ball, the team form a ruck to try to win the ball back, trying to ruck the ball back with their feet.

10. **Maul**
    If a ball carrier is held up (a tackle which doesn't bring the player to the ground) a maul may form, when players can only join the maul from behind their team-mates and not come in from the side.

11. **Line-out**
    If the ball goes out of the field of play, into touch, a line-out restarts the game. Players from both teams form parallel lines while the ball is thrown down the middle of the line-out from the touch line and players are lifted by their team-mates in an effort to win the ball.

12. **Scrum**
    If a player infringes the rules, for example by being offside, a scrum may be awarded, where the eight forwards from each team bind together and push against the opposition to win the ball, which is fed in down the centre of the tunnel.

HOW TO BE FABULOUS
AT THE RUGBY...

Follow our simple guide to rugby style and you'll soon have a whole new perspective on the game.

- The atmosphere before any big game is part of the fun. Make sure you get there early. And starting the match-day party with a champagne picnic means it won't really matter if you know the rules or not!

- While you want to look gorgeous, you also want to be warm. Invest in a striking full-length coat and matching scarf and gloves.

- It's chilly in the stands and the weather can never be trusted – make sure your make-up is weatherproof.

- Indulge the trend for girly wellingtons or pretty ballet shoes, as sky-scraper heels may start to pinch. Especially if your team is winning and you're leaping up and down enthusiastically!

- Be ready to join in – sing as loud as you can in support of your team, cheer on the tries and allow yourself to get into the spirit of it all. You'll be surprised at how much fun you have!

- Not sure whether you'll enjoy the game? Check out Rugby Sevens. Group tournaments are played all around the UK throughout the year, and with only seven men on the pitch.

- Rugby supporters are a jolly bunch. There are many new friends to be had over a beer and a hog roast!

- A rugby game is only eighty minutes long. Why stop the afternoon there? Plan a fabulous after party and play perfect hostess.

ROMANTIC RUGBY

What better excuse than the six countries of the Six Nations to treat yourself and your partner to a romantic weekend away! You can share the fun of a match and then enjoy a new city together.

In *At the Argentinean Billionaire's Bidding*, Tamsin is forced to follow playboy Alejandro to his home city of **Buenos Aires**. While the Argentinean team are not *strictly* part of the Six Nations competition, do you need an excuse to visit the legendary home of the tango? You might want more than a romantic weekend to investigate all that this stunning country has to offer.

Explore some more of the amazing countryside; Argentina boasts the world's southernmost city, huge waterfalls, the continent's only advancing glaciers, ski slopes, beaches, golf courses, polo clubs, and the widest river estuary on the planet. Alternatively, learn to play polo and enjoy an *asado* (an Argentinean barbecue).

Visit **Iguazu Falls**, one of the most popular tourist attractions in Argentina. Legend has it that a god planned to marry a beautiful aborigine named Naipí, who fled with her mortal lover Tarobá in a canoe. In rage, the god sliced the river creating the waterfalls, condemning the lovers to an eternal fall.

Behind the scenes with the England team

While you settle yourself in the stands and the build-up to the kick-off begins, what has been happening behind the scenes? The England team doctor tells us:

As the doctor I see all the players when they arrive at training camp – I see and assess their injuries, and then with the physiotherapists and the massage therapists I work out what treatment plans we need to do for them. Some players when they arrive are so injured that they're not going to be able to play for us, in which case they sometimes return to their club for treatment. It's a lot of work when you first get together, because all of a sudden thirty players descend and most rugby players are a little bit injured most of the time. And then as the week goes on, having set up those treatment plans, we deliver massage treatment, physio treatment, rehab treatment for those players whilst the other group train. Then they play the game at the weekend and we start all over again!

Every day the medical hours are really long. The medical team – which is me, two physiotherapists, a massage therapist – meet for breakfast at 7am and we open the medical treatment room at around 7.15am, and then we pretty much have it open all the way through to the evening meeting at 10pm, at which time we go to bed. There are only two breaks!

Match days are really fun though. The medical team has a ritual: everyone goes training at 7am and then we massage players, strap players and the physios leave very early with Dave Tennison, the kit man, to get everything sorted in the changing room. I come down on the bus with the players and before the game I help physios strap shoulders, listen to the last-minute team talk, make sure that I've got my medical bag sorted out, check my microphone and that my headset is working and get ready to work pitchside.

Running out onto the pitch I fight between the emotion of the moment and the need to be very considered in what I do. First, am I going to be in danger by entering the pitch at this time and be run over by another player? Then, when you get to the player, loads of questions run through my head before I look at shoulders, knees and ankles and so on. It's difficult because the referees always want to make the game carry on.

One of the worst injuries I've ever had to deal with was a broken ankle – he's such a tough player that initially he thought he would be able to walk off the field and we had a bit of an argument, where I insisted he wouldn't be able to and needed to go off on a stretcher and he was clearly in a great deal of pain but wasn't showing it! Once or twice I've had players that have dislocated their shoulders and if possible you try and put a shoulder back there and then on the pitch.

After the game is when our work really starts. We examine and assess everybody and usually start treating people that evening.

I think my job is the best job there is in sports medicine. It's a fantastic job and I've been privileged to do it for six years and it's always been an ambition since I first came to Twickenham to watch some rugby – it's a great job.

Fixture list

The **RBS 6 Nations** starts in February 2009!
Inspired to follow the England team? Here are the
fixture dates for your diary.

Date of match	Kick-off		Location
Sat 7th Feb 09	15:00	England v Italy	Twickenham
Sat 7th Feb 09	17:00	Ireland v France	Croke Park
Sun 8th Feb 09	15:00	Scotland v Wales	Murrayfield
Sat 14th Feb 09	16:00	France v Scotland	Stade de France
Sat 14th Feb 09	17:30	Wales v England	Millennium Stadium
Sun 15th Feb 09	15:30	Italy v Ireland	Stadio Flaminio
Fri 27th Feb 09	21:00	France v Wales	Stade de France
Sat 28th Feb 09	15:00	Scotland v Italy	Murrayfield
Sat 28th Feb 09	17:30	Ireland v England	Croke Park
Sat 14th Mar 09	16:00	Italy v Wales	Stadio Flaminio
Sat 14th Mar 09	17:00	Scotland v Ireland	Murrayfield
Sun 15th Mar 09	15:00	England v France	Twickenham
Sat 21st Mar 09	14:15	Italy v France	Stadio Flaminio
Sat 21st Mar 09	15:30	England v Scotland	Twickenham
Sat 21st Mar 09	17:30	Wales v Ireland	Millennium Stadium

Coming next month from

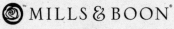
MILLS & BOON®

and

ENGLAND
RUGBY

a sexy French boss!

The French Tycoon's Pregnant Mistress

by

Abby Green

Read on for a sneak preview…

"With a nail-biting finish like that, I think we can safely say that this tournament is wide open and set to be one of the most exciting yet. This is Alana Cusack reporting live from Croke Park, back to you in the studio, Brian."

Alana kept the smile pasted on her face until she could hear the chatter die away in her ear-piece and then handed her microphone to her assistant, Aisling, with relief once she knew she was off air. She avoided looking to where she knew the man was still standing, his shoulder propped non-chalantly against the wall, hands in the pockets of his dark trousers, underneath a black overcoat with the collar turned up. He'd been talking to one of the French players but now he was alone again.

He was watching her. And he'd been watching her all through the Six Nations match between Ireland and France. He'd unsettled her and he'd distracted her. And she didn't know why.

That was a lie, she knew exactly why. He was dark and brooding and so gorgeous that when she'd first locked eyes with him, quite by accident, it felt as though someone had just punched her in the stomach. There had been an instant tug of recognition and *something* very alien and disconcerting. Certainly something that no other man had ever made her feel.

Not even her husband.

The tug had been so strong that she'd felt herself smiling and raising a quizzical brow, but then she'd seen an unmistakably mocking glint in his dark eyes. Of course she didn't know him, she'd never seen his long, hard-boned face before, never seen that mouth which, even from where she sat, had the most amazingly sensuous lips. Immediately she'd felt herself flushing at her reaction to him.

He had to be French, as he shared the quintessential good looks of so many of the crowd today. Quite exotically different to the more pale-skinned home crowd of Irish supporters. And he'd been sitting in the seats reserved for VIPs, situated just below the press area. He looked like a VIP. She'd only had to look once to know that he had effortlessly stood out from the rest of the crowd. But her gaze had been inexorably drawn to him again and again, and to her utter mortification their eyes had met more than once. When he'd stood intermittently with the crowd during a try or a conversion, he'd stood taller and broader than any of the men around him and in a crowd full of rugby supporters that was something.

Yet was he waiting now because he thought that she'd been giving him some sort of come-on? Everything in Alana clammed up and rejected that thought. She would never be so blatant.

INTERNATIONAL BILLIONAIRES

WIN A LUXURY WEEKEND IN LONDON!

We've got a luxury weekend stay at the Home of England Rugby up for grabs in every edition of the International Billionaires mini-series (x 8).

You and a partner will be treated to two nights' accommodation in the brand-new London Marriott Hotel Twickenham, where you'll receive a free tour of the famous stadium, as well as entry to the World Rugby Museum.

TWICKENHAM WORLD RUGBY MUSEUM & STADIUM TOURS

Marriott LONDON TWICKENHAM

You'll also each come away with a free goody bag, packed with books, England Rugby clothing and other accessories.

INTERNATIONAL BILLIONAIRES

To enter, complete the entry form below and send to:
Mills & Boon RFU/March Prize Draw,
Eton House, 18-24 Paradise Road,
Richmond, Surrey, TW9 1SR

Mills & Boon® Rugby Prize Draw (March)

Name: _____

Address: _____

Post Code: _____

Daytime Telephone No: _____

E-mail Address: _____

❑ I have read the terms and conditions (please tick this box before entering).

❑ Please tick here if you do not wish to receive special offers from
Harlequin Mills & Boon Ltd.

Closing date for entries is 19th April 2009

Terms & Conditions

1. Draw open to UK and Eire residents aged 18 and over. No purchase necessary. One entry per household per prize draw only. 2. Prizes are non-transferable and no cash alternatives will be offered. 3. All travel expenses to and from Twickenham must be covered by the prize winner. 4. All prizes are subject to availability. Should any prize be unavailable, a prize of similar value will be substituted. 5. Employees and immediate family members of Harlequin Mills & Boon Ltd are not eligible to enter. 6. Prize winners will be randomly selected from the eligible entries received. No correspondence will be entered into and no entry returned. 7. To be eligible, all entries must be received by 19th April 2009. 8. Prize-winner notification will be made by e-mail or letter no later than 15 days after the deadline for entry. 9. No responsibility can be accepted for entries that are lost, delayed or damaged. Proof of postage cannot be accepted as proof of delivery. 10. If any winner notification or prize is returned as undeliverable, an alternative winner will be drawn from eligible entries. 11. Names of competition winners are available on request.

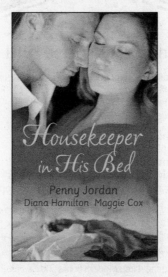

FREE!

4 Books
and a surprise gift!

·We would like to take this opportunity to thank you for reading this Mills & Boon® book by offering you the chance to take FOUR more specially selected titles from the Modern™ series absolutely FREE! We're also making this offer to introduce you to the benefits of the Mills & Boon® Book Club™—

- ★ FREE home delivery
- ★ FREE gifts and competitions
- ★ FREE monthly Newsletter
- ★ Exclusive Mills & Boon Book Club offers
- ★ Books available before they're in the shops

Accepting these FREE books and gift places you under no obligation to buy, you may cancel at any time, even after receiving your free shipment. Simply complete your details below and return the entire page to the address below. You don't even need a stamp!

YES! Please send me 4 free Modern books and a surprise gift. I understand that unless you hear from me, I will receive 6 superb new titles every month for just £3.19 each, postage and packing free. I am under no obligation to purchase any books and may cancel my subscription at any time. The free books and gift will be mine to keep in any case.

P9ZEF

Ms/Mrs/Miss/Mr .... Initials ....
                                                        BLOCK CAPITALS PLEASE
Surname ....
Address ....
....
.... Postcode ....

Send this whole page to:
UK: FREEPOST CN81, Croydon, CR9 3WZ